# THE CRUCIFIXION

ALSO BY ISMITH KHAN

*The Jumbie Bird*
*The Obeah Man*
*A Day in the Country*

ISMITH KHAN

# THE CRUCIFIXION

PEEPAL TREE

First published in Great Britain in 1987
Reprinted 2007
Peepal Tree Press Ltd
17 King's Avenue
Leeds LS6 1QS
UK





ISBN 13: 9780948833045

Peepal Tree gratefully acknowledges Arts Council support

There was nothing that Manko wished for that did not come his way. He sat in his little hut many an evening after he had finished his supper of dried codfish and ground provisions, and asked himself if there was anything he truly wanted. He thought of the possessions of other men, and he had no envy of them. And surveying his simple belongings, he went even a step further, asking himself if he really needed them; could he not get along without this pot or that pan, or some other utensil? He played a kind of game with himself, and he was always pleased to come out the winner, someone who did not crave things, who did not carp about not having them, and someone who did not break his back like other men to own and possess things which they soon tired of anyway.

Yet, as pleased as he was with himself for coming out the winner in the games be played, he was still left with a kind of disappointment, a vague hollow feeling that something was missing. It was a feeling he always knew, even as a boy. As far back as he could remember, he had asked himself what he needed to make his body and being complete, and even as he grew up he tried to strip himself of things so that he could see how well he could manage without them, and he could remember no time that he wanted anything except that day when he first met the preacher.

Although he did not work and persevere like other young men in the village, he was not lazy. Often some villager would ask him to help out in clearing a field, or ploughing up a piece of land. Another would ask him to put in a few days building some chicken coops, and he never refused. He never asked like other men, 'How much you goin' to pay me?' He simply went along the following day and set to work, and worked even more diligently than helpers who would skulk about, and demand hot lunches and a nip of rum to wash down the food and then went to sleep in the heat of the afternoon, only to demand their wages when the job was done. Manko, on the other hand, was given a bottle of rum, or a few hands of bananas, sometimes a sackful of ground provisions, or permission to pluck mangoes or oranges from the trees in the yard of the villager he had helped out. And he did not seem strange to the villagers, they looked upon him as a kind of saint, for he had none of the wild ways of the young men of the village. When the day came for his life to burst open and explode like a calabash in the sun, all the villagers knew that he had heard the call; some went so far as to say that they knew all along that he was a messenger of the Lord sent to dwell among them.

But Manko did not think anything of the kind, he merely followed his instincts, his restlessness; his life carried him along a tide that he did not question. All of the things that he ever needed seemed to walk into his life, even the thing he loved most, and cared for above all other things, had simply flown into his life one day. He was awakened one morning by a voice calling from outside his hut. "Wake up! Wake up! ...Time to wake up!" He was still half asleep as he went to the window. Was he dreaming? The little yard was empty. He turned to go back to bed and there it was again. "Wake up! Wake up! ...Time to wake up!" The voice seemed to come from the tumbledown small lemon tree which grew wild beside the hut, and perched on one of its branches was a small green parrot.

"Who you tryin' to wake up?" Manko asked the bird, but it only replied as before, "Wake up! Wake up!... Time to wake up!"

He got a ripe banana and peeled it, then he went out to the bird, stepping lightly and speaking fondly as he approached, and when he got close to it, the bird jumped onto his wrist and began eating the banana. Manko felt so happy that he stroked the bird's head, and the bird fluffed out its feathers in a corolla about its neck, sidestepping one foot after the other until it was perched on his shoulder. He was afraid to move at first, but when he did, the bird remained there. "Say Manko!" he told the bird, and with a quickness that appalled him, the bird repeated his name. "Now say Lorrito," he told the bird, and the bird repeated this name, which all parrots are given, with great rapidity. Manko was delighted with the thought of teaching the bird to speak. He knew that Lorrito must have an owner, and he feared during the first few days that it would fly away to its home; perhaps someone would see him walking about with the parrot on his shoulder and claim it.

But days went past, and the bird seemed happy to be with him. He never chained it at night to prevent it from running away, and though one day he saw a beautiful bird cage which he was tempted to get for Lorrito, again, he did not want to cage the bird; it was his only friend, and he loved to teach it new words and sentences, for the bird quickly learnt to speak with the deep, rich intonations of Manko's voice.

And so, he would place the parrot on his shoulder and go to the junction. Saturday night was always the big night for him. Everyone on the sugar estate got paid on Saturday, and went to the junction where there were a few shops, stores, a rumshop, and hundreds of peddlers who spread out their goods on the ground. There were ice-cream vendors, and deep-fried pig's feet, there were people selling potions for growing hair, tonics for weak brains, and under the awning of the rumshop there was a preacher in a white robe with a banana leaf in front of him where his listeners placed cents and pennies as the preacher swept his arm about and shot out his accusing finger at one person or another.

Manko was fourteen when he first came upon the preacher, and even then he could see how the preacher was a reader of the minds of men, for each time the preacher made an accusation and then threatened some culprit with the fires of hell, someone came forward and paid up. 'The man just like me... He does see things just the way I see them,' Manko thought to himself. The preacher had let his hair grow long, and his beard was ragged and unkempt and Manko began rubbing his chin, for he felt that to look like a preacher was an asset; it made him look holy, it made him look as if he had held conversations with God. Manko stood off to the sides listening to the preacher many Saturdays before he finally got up the nerve and courage to approach him.

"Where you could get a book like that?" he asked the preacher, pointing to the Bible which lay open on a banana leaf surrounded by coins. The preacher looked up at him, then turned away. Manko stood waiting for an answer.

"You know how to read?" the preacher asked. His voice was sullen and filled with disdain. He as much as told Manko that he would forever be a fool because he did not know how to read.

"I could learn," Manko said in his half-boy's, half-man's voice. He knew that to speak up to the preacher man-to-man would only get him insults, but if he sounded like a fool, the preacher would take time and patience with him, and the preacher did.

"You want to learn the works of the Lord God?" Manko did not know anything about that, he only knew that he loved the spell the preacher cast over the small clique, and he loved the way the man was dressed, but he answered yes anyway.

The preacher went into a long rigmarole about fasting, staying clean, staying away from almost everything, and Manko felt that the man was only trying to discourage him. He listened with rapt attention though, because he could see how much he had moved the preacher by his questions, and he had long ago learnt that if you wanted anything from anyone, you became a good listener, because people loved to talk and brag about themselves. But when the preacher finally said to him, "...and the most important thing is ...that you have to hear the call!" Manko felt a cold chill run through him, for it was the one thing he had not heard. He asked the preacher how and when and where he had heard the call, but the man was evasive. "When the Good Lord call pan you, you bounds and determined to know his voice... You is a young man still, and God aint have time with young people nowadays. But you could listen... Listen, and if he call you, then you know what road cut out for you."

So he had many things to learn. He remembered how the hours lingered on in the classroom as a child repeating 'A for Apple, B for Bat, C for Cat, D for Dog.' Now suddenly all of those hours and days no longer seemed like the waste they did; he found that he remembered all of his reading lessons. He did not know how to spell, so he spent his time going over the big words two or three times until he knew them. And then there was knowledge, and who had that? The old man who hung around the rumshop? Everyone called him 'philosopher'. Manko worked up enough courage and boldness to approach the old man one day.

"I want some knowledge," he said to the old man as though he were in the shop to buy a tin of milk, and the old man replied to him in kind. "You go have to pay!"

"How much?"

"Well what you want to know?"

"I want to know who make the sea and what it make out of."

"That go cost you four cents," the philosopher said firmly. Manko dug into his fob pocket and looked at the three cents he had; the philosopher looked at the three cents also and a look of disappointment came over his face. Manko turned his eyes up to him pleadingly, and the old man said, "You could owe me the cent." Manko nodded and the philosopher began.

"God pull out this piece of a thing we call the world from the sun and he roll it up in he hand and pelt it out in the sky like a cricket ball... just like that," the old man said, hurling his arm through the air like a bowler, then he pushed the three cents to the bar-keeper who brought him a shot of dark rum which he swallowed in one gulp and then he started again.

"One day God get news from one of the angels bout what a bad place the world was, and he came down to see, and when he see how evil the people was, he begin to cry, and that is how the sea get make, and that is why it taste so salty." Manko looked amazed at the old man.

"I want to know about the sky."

"That will cost you five cents," the philosopher told him firmly.

"I will come back tomorrow," said Manko as he walked away in deep thought. How long ago all this happened, how many times the old man had told him threateningly that knowledge had to be paid for, and how many times Manko went on with his pressing questions to the old man he could not remember; but he did get knowledge; the philosopher had told him so himself before he died in the rumshop that day when he took on a bet that he could drink a bottle of rum without once removing it from his lips. He won the bet all right, but he fell dead right on the spot, and Manko had to search elsewhere for knowledge. The only other person he was sure had any knowledge was the preacher.

Manko went back time and again to listen to the preacher. At first he was enveloped in the spell the man cast over his little congregation, carried away by the preacher's gesturing, and the sounds the words from the Bible made in his head. He longed to speak like that, to pull out words from the Bible, hurl them at people and watch them cower. He spent his days waiting and longing for Saturday night when he could go to the junction to observe all the preacher's actions and gestures.

One evening he saw the preacher picking up the money, and he watched the greedy and hungry look in his eyes as he collected the offering from the banana leaf. After he pocketed all the money, the preacher picked up one coin, tested it between his teeth, pounded it with a stone, then began cursing under his breath. He looked up suddenly and saw Manko staring at him.

He was about to curse, but instead he threw the bogus coin at Manko.

"Here boy, see if you can't pass this bad money on somebody. It go look bad if they catch a holy man like me trying to pass bad money." Then he cursed the villain who left it in the offering. Manko's hand flung out, and he caught the coin. As he rolled it between his fingers, he did not so much think of passing it off on someone as he thought that he had caught the preacher; he had seen him, he had learnt something of much greater value than any coin. He simply felt that when his turn came, he would be a much better preacher, because he could see behind the veils that men cover themselves with, and this was his gift, the gift of the lonely, the solitary. He studied men, he knew men, he would be a preacher, he had only to hear the call. He was not going to be as foolish as the preacher. He was clever, he examined his thoughts. Where the preacher was like a beast of the jungle following instinct blindly, he, Manko, would put himself in the kind of place that God was likely to look for him. And where was that? Why, Port of Spain, of course. Where were all the rumshops? Where were all the rogues and rascals? They were certainly not in the bush, they were all in the city. A man could wait out his life in the wrong place, listening to the wrong things, but that was not for Manko, he would wait until he heard the 'call', then he would begin. He had spent his whole life becoming, now it was time to be.

As the days went by, Manko worked himself into a feverish

state; his brain felt light, and his body sweated, and he felt in God's presence. When he stopped for a moment and felt tired or depressed, he asked God to speak, to let him know that he had been called. Looking out of the window of his hut, he would say with Biblical intonations, "If I see a black and white horse go pas' between now an the time the estate whistle blow... God call 'pan me." And before the day was over, he had seen the horse go by. At another time, there were some small lizards racing about the floor of the hut. He closed his eyes and counted to ten. If the lizards were still there, God wanted him. He asked God to speak to him in a dream and that night he dreamt that someone was calling him from the street. It was God's voice! He woke up in the middle of the night and said to himself that if he looked out of the window and saw a fire out in the sugarcane fields which surrounded his hut, then he would know. He got up and looked out, and there it was, fire. It was the end of the crop season when the dead stalks were set on fire and their ashes returned to the ground to fertilize the earth. Fire was fire, and a sign was a sign. Why should he tax God? He wanted only to please God, and make his task, his signs simpler.

*Now, it have a way they teach we how to write a book in school and it have a way we have to write a book if we want to write a book about a certain kinda people who come from a certain kinda place.*

*So, Manko, who want to be a preacher, ask for a sign, he ask for so many signs, he ask God to talk wid him and he t'ink that God talk wid him. Whether God is a man, who is white-man or a black-man, whether God livin' somewhere upstairs in the sky, or whether God is somebody who does ride a bicycle, drive a moto-car, buy a big house up in Saint Ann's an' Saint Clair we don't know, but what we go talk about is what happen to the preacher.*

*The preacher was a fella who come from a small town in de islan'. He know what he know, and he know what he know because the only t'ing he know is the kinda t'ing that people tell him. They tell him, "If ya straighten up, boy, you could make you way in the world." They tell him, "If you learn how to read and write you could make somet'ing of youself in the world." They tell him that if he's a good boy, he boun' to make out all right. And the preacher, Manko, was a fella who like to listen to people because he want to learn some damn t'ing.*

*The boy went to school and he went up to fourth standard. And then the boy went to the orphanage because he whole family disappear. And when he went to the orphanage they give him a uniform, and they give him a Bible and it had other boys in the orphanage who get the same uniform, they get the same Bible, and some of them get a musical instrument. They teach them how to blow a trumpet and how to play a saxophone and how to play a kettle drum and how to play a big-drum and how to play a tuba. And when they didn't play good, they would bus' a lash in dey ass.*

*On Tuesday evenings you could always go and hear a band concert in Woodford Square where it have a nice little bandstand, some people call it a grandstand, is a very nice lookin' place, like a little umbrella with all kinda ironwork around it and it sittin' on top of a cement kinda ring about four five feet high and it use to have a lotta fellas, for example, who use to take their girlfriend to listen to the band concert, though they didn't take them to listen to the band concert, they take them to listen to somet'ing else, a quiet little corner in a place behind the park, where they could do what both of them know they come here to do.*

*But to get back to Manko, he had he uniform and he had he Bible and while he didn't learn how to play an instrument, he use to have to go along there. It was a pleasure to watch them boys come out o' that van. They was really well trained, they was so damn well behaved. The bandmaster would come out and the boys would come outa the van and they would stand up outside Woodford Square in a nice row, and then the bandmaster would tell them to turn left or turn right and hold they instruments properly and then they would walk in single file up into the bandstand. They even use to have in them days, in front of the bandstand, one of them t'ings that look like a shiel', that they would stick in the ground that would have the music on it, and they use to make those boys in the orphanage polish it up so that it would look nice and shining. Anyway, that is what happen if you have to go to the orphanage, so when you come out, you come out right, you goin' to do all o' the right t'ings. So, this is what Manko went t'rough when he family die.*

*He was a damn good boy. Everybody in the village like him. Why? They like him because he use to do all kinda little t'ings for them, help them out here and there and he never ask for too much. Now, somet'ing happen to this boy, maybe one of the masters in the orphanage bus' a lash in he head one day and it affec' he senses. Maybe the boy was just a chupid boy. When he come out from the orphanage, the boy went back to the town where he family come from, but all of them disappear. The boy lookin' for somet'ing. Now, some a' you might t'ink is a chupid kinda t'ing to say that a boy like this lookin' for somet'ing, only white people lookin' for somet'ing, not black people.*

*But, he lookin, and he lookin' and he lookin' and what the hell he find? He try to get a job. He aint have no education. He try to go look for a work by the airlines. Everybody know that the only people who could get a work there go have to be white people who know how to read and write and who would sell tickets to tourists. The boy go work for a doctor one time. And the damn doctor tell him, he say, "Listen, boy, if you come in here and you sweep up the place every morning, I goin' to teach you how to be a doctor." The boy so damn chupid, he believe the doctor, and he went to work for him. He really believe that this man would teach him how to do doctor-work. He didn't know that if you goin' to be a doctor, you have to go away some damn place, far away, where it have snow, where you have to have a lotta money, where you have to study, where you have to read books. He really believe that the man would teach him how to be a doctor. So he sweep up the place, he do a lotta t'ings. And then he went back and say, "I have to do somet'ing, I have to do somet'ing with me life." That is what he was saying when he say, "I have to hear the voice of God." That is what he saying when he ask heself, "What de ass I going to do wid me life?" It have somet'ing in some o' them fellas like this boy, who want to know some damn t'ing. What to do wid theyself, how to make a lotta money, what de ass we doing here, where de hell the world come from... Well, you could go on and on.*

*Manko want to know some damn t'ing, somet'ing that would give him a little bit o' peace of mind, some people would call it. He want to do somet'ing wid he life. Now, is very hard to find a job in Trinidad. Is very hard, even if you find a job, to keep the damn job. Is very hard even if you find the job and keep the job, to understand why-the-ass you take the job in the firs' place. Is very hard to understan' a lotta t'ings that a lotta people in a lotta different, different, part of the world understand. But Trinidadians born chupid, so that is the way they t'ink.*

*So he ax for a sign, he ax for God to come down. Black people doubt. White people doubt. Orphanage boy proof? He want to know some damn t'ing. And even he didn't know what that t'ing was. But they teach him how to read and write in the orphanage. And the only book they teach him how to read was the Bible, so that is what he know. And you can't blame a man for operatin' inside o' that circle if he come from a place like that. He have a certain number o' tools, he get them in the orphanage, he get them in the island. But it still have somet'ing else in the man. He don't want jus' to see time passin, he want to do somet'ing wid he life. So he have he tools, though he's not a carpenter, he's not a shoemaker. It use to have a lotta boys in the orphanage who they teach carpentering and shoemaking, and when they didn't straighten up, they would bus' a lash in dey ass, but somehow or other somebody look at Manko and say, "Dis boy look like if he should be in Bible class." He didn't know how to play music. He use to like to listen to music but he don't have any talents in that direction. But he have this chupid t'ing that use to wake him up in the middle of the night, somet'ing that use to say, "Listen boy, you come into dis damn world, you goin' to go out o' it, you have to make somet'ing o' you life you know." Manko was asking this all over again, "What-de-ass to do wid meself?" You could call that boredom, man. It have a special word for it in the Caribbean. If you meet a fella like Manko, the first t'ing somebody would say, "Listen, ya damn idler, why the hell ya don't go out and find a job?" Well the boy did try to find a job and the boy did work at the job and the boy was still asking this same damn question, "What-de-ass to do wid meself?"*

*Why-the-hell a man can't come into the world and have a good time and go out of it? Why he have to ask heself all the time what to do wid heself? Why Manko, who come from a tiny place like this island, want to do this? If you ask Manko if he really think that, he would be the first one to tell you, "Boy, I don't understand t'ings like dat. I understand one t'ing only and that is dat God call pon me. I ax him to show me he face, he show he face and I say one t'ing, God call me."*

And then came that Saturday when the preacher did not appear. Manko was filled with an excitement that could not be quenched. He went through the shops, he mingled among the wayside vendors inquiring whether they knew what had happened to the preacher. No one knew. His heart and body pained and longed for something, something which had transported him and calmed him on Saturday evenings. Now it was gone. Was this a sign? Was this God's way of calling upon him? He felt restless and the evening seemed incomplete. He knew that if he went home he would only lie in bed, restless and tossing. He walked back to see if the preacher was there, and looking at the empty spot where the preacher usually stood, Manko felt drawn to it. He walked over and stood on the spot, and his body went limp and cold. He cast his eyes up to heaven, then closed them, waiting for a sign. Anything that God did or said he would welcome now. "If a bolt of lightning shoot cross the sky," he thought, "if a big wind come down and sweep past my face, if a branch break loose with a crack! A leaf?" he pleaded with heaven. "Let a leaf fall down and then I will know that God call me." He opened his eyes, and there in front of him, from a tall mango tree came sailing down one of its long, dry slender leaves. Manko's heart leapt, and he ran to the leaf, looking at it with reverence, then he knelt down slowly and picked it up and went home. He read his Bible, he thought of the sign that God had sent him, and after a day or two, he began wanting more, he wanted to hear God's voice call out to him.

He had read in the Bible about times when God's voice had come like a mighty roar of thunder out of the skies, and at times he came close to threatening God to speak to him, but he was filled with the fear of the consequences. What if God did not speak? If he wished for the signs of the lizards on the floor, the sight of the black and white horse before evening, a fire in the fields, and they all came to pass, he could perhaps slowly increase his demands on God. All would come later. In the meantime, he was pleased with the little signs that God had shown him, telling him in small ways that he, Manko, had been called. God had his reasons, and who knew what they were? Perhaps God was not ready to show his face yet, to hurl down his mighty voice among the thunder bolts. And then, sparked by a sudden revelation, Manko asked himself, "Suppose God aint want to talk to me like a common man?" What if he wore his long white robe and held his Bible and read God's word to the four winds? Then God might speak!

"Next Saturday, please God," he said to himself, "I goin' to get dress-up in my robes, hold my Bible in my hand in that same spot in the junction where I know God done come and talk to people already... I bounds and determine to hear He voice."

And so during the week he prepared himself, body and soul. He read aloud from the great Bible, and chose a section from the book of Job which he rehearsed in front of his shaving mirror. He lifted his eyebrows, he lowered them, he leaned far backwards, then pitched forward. He held his hands up in the air, he held them to his temples until he had all the gestures he needed to fit each line of the psalm he would hurl at the people in the junction.

His beard and his hair were of fair length; he was not as impressive as his mentor, but then the Good Lord in his youth looked that way too, and Manko did not feel that his appearance was lacking. He wore a long white robe, and let his finger nails grow long. The preacher's were always black and unclean, but Manko saw where he could improve on the preacher's appearance. He would let his fingernails grow long, (though he never did understand why this had to be done), but he felt deep within himself that his nails had to be cleaned and scraped. The Lord spoke in many ways, but man went unheeding. At each turn of the way, there was God's voice, and Manko heard that voice speaking to him. Questions turned over in his mind. Should he get himself a pair of sandals, or should he go barefooted? And before long God had spoken to him: "Wear sandals!" The other preacher went about barefooted, and it was clear to Manko that God wanted him, Manko, to be an even more diligent servant.

As he stood before the small clique of worshippers at the junction that evening, his limbs trembled and his voice quavered with fear and trembling for the 'spirit'. They were convinced that the power of God was strong in this man, that his voice trembled because of his faith and conviction, and they punctuated his statements with "Amen, Amen." Manko read from his great Bible with even more zest. His voice began to lose its tremor and he now had to create it deliberately as he read a line from the Bible, stopped, and then went on to interpret it freely. The little clique reached the size where it could no longer be ignored. People who did not ordinarily bother to come and listen to a preacher came to see why the crowd had gathered, and then stayed and listened. Coins were dropping on his offering cloth, and he longed to look down to see how many were copper and how many silver, but he forced himself to look heavenward, his voice rolling back and forth like the ebb and flow of an incoming tide, pressing closer and closer ahead with each successive wave.

He thought how the older preacher came right out and accused people, frightened and threatened them with God's painful tortures and punishments. He remembered how the old preacher swung about and pointed directly at a man or a woman, spelt out their sin, then went through the pages of the Bible and found the punishment that God had laid down for them, but Manko was not going to imitate that kind of threatening sermon filled with hell and fire and demons. He turned his eyes to heaven saying, "Don't think that God aint see you... He have eyes that bigger than the sea, and ears that have more strength and power than the telephone! He see you, and He hear you, and He ask you to come up here tonight and ask for His forgiveness." And come up they did, and ask for forgiveness they did, pay up they did, as Manko held his head high, his eyes turned away from the sinners as they came forward to drop their offering on the cloth.

Meantime Manko tilted his head to heaven with his eyes closed, pleading with God to show himself. "Look at how all these people come here tonight to hear your words. Lord, look at how your servant Manko make them see the light... That is the way I want to hear your voice, talking to me, so that I will know that you call me up. Is not a big thing that I asking for, Lord; I is a quiet man. I not asking for moto' car, or bicycle, or big house. I don't want to ask you for acres pon acres of land like some people, I only want to hear your voice," he said to himself.

The strength and power of his words had so moved him that when he came to the last sentence, he opened his eyes and began saying them aloud to the congregation: "I only want to hear your voice... I only want to hear your voice... I only want to hear your voice." The worshippers answered, "Amen... Amen," and some of them picked up the rhythm and intonation of his voice, the rise and fall of his tone, and they too began repeating after him "I only want to hear your voice."

Then Manko said, "Speak to me, Lord... speak to me." And the congregation answered, "I only want to hear your voice... I only want to hear your voice." Their bodies swayed and rocked from a deep compulsion within. Lorrito, Manko's parrot, perched on his shoulder, also picked up the rhythm and refrain. Now he repeated, "I only want to hear your voice," then later, "Speak to me, Lord... speak to me, Lord," and as Manko changed the accent in the sentence, stressing the word **'speak'**, so did Lorrito change his accenting, saying, 'Speak'. Manko's eyes were still clamped shut and his hands poised in front of him in prayer and meditation. He heard a grumbling in the crowd, and the bird's wings fluttered against his cheek as it cried out, "Speak... speak... speak." Manko opened his eyes and saw someone forcing his way through the crowd. The man was saying, "Speak, eh! Speak, eh! You want to hear me speak?" as he pushed people left and right to get close to Manko. The bird began to caw from excitement, and Manko had to calm it down by stroking the feathers along its head and back. The interruption broke the spell he had cast with his words, and his heart began to beat faster. Either he had picked up a feeling of danger from Lorrito, or Lorrito had picked it up from him, but now they were both excited when the man suddenly broke through the front row of the crowd and swung a crashing blow on Manko's head. It was, he saw in the instant before the blow found its mark, the old preacher.

"You nasty little thief... you gone and thief my spot!"

Reaction in the crowd was confused; everything had happened so quickly. Most of the worshippers who got pushed and shoved by the old preacher thought it was someone whose spirit was so moved that he could no longer contain himself and had to rush to the feet of Manko and lie there prostrate until he was purged. Some were so shocked and stunned at the sight of one holy man striking another that it took moments before anger rose up in them.

"But what is things comin' to nowadays?" a man in the front rows asked his neighbour.

"The old man is a crook," he answered. "You never see him here before?"

"So why he dress up like a priest, then?"

"To fool chupid people... What else? The man is a bogus priest, where you ever hear bout one priest hitting the other? I listen to that young priest ask God to come and talk with him, and I know that he is a holy man."

Manko meantime lay flat on the ground looking up at the

angry face of the old preacher. The parrot was thrown from his shoulder and stood squawking a few feet away, smoothing out its feathers which were twisted out of place by the sudden jolt. And as the bird preened its feathers, it still shouted, as the congregation had shouted before, "Speak.. speak." Manko looked at the bird with a kind of hurt and shame. He felt that the bird should not see him humiliated this way, and he tried to get up. But the old man was much more powerful than he, and pushed him down again.

"You is a bogus priest!" someone shouted from the crowd. The old preacher turned to look for the voice. He had come here week after week to save them; they had gone away cleansed and blessed by him; how could they now turn against him? Was that the way people were? Was this one of the men who was part of his flock?

"You only playin' priest till you bounce up with a real priest!" another voice called. Before the old preacher turned to look amongst the faces of the congregation again, he looked at Manko threateningly. "You better stop right where you is! Try to get up, and see if I aint lick you down!"

Manko's face was hurt and pained. He thought of how the Lord was beaten and humiliated before his crucifixion, and Manko felt his pain. He imagined the suffering Christ had suffered; his body ached, his eyes rolled up in their sockets, and his lids fell slowly shut. Then he began speaking softly, "The Lord is my shepherd... I shall not want. He leadeth me..."

The old preacher was infuriated as he heard the words of the psalm... his psalm. Manko had stolen that, too. Manko's intense feeling of defeat and resignation made the words of the psalm new and different... It was as though the congregation had never heard those words before and they struck at the old preacher like physical blows. He wanted to slap Manko, stop his mouth so that he could not finish the recitation. He rolled up his fist and drew back his hand to strike Manko down, to stun him once and for all.

But Manko remained lying on the ground, still, silent, and suffering. He had only to read aloud, or think hard of words and deeds in the Bible now, and he became immersed in them. He felt, thought and acted out the expressions of martyr and saint, and if true emotion is any test of sincerity, then Manko was sincere, for he felt pain and hurt and grief; he became that saint or martyr, and knew with his own senses and his own body all the things that they had known, and this was clear to his congregation as it spilled over from him like a great cloud enveloping anyone who came close and heard the words of God spoken through his voice. The old preacher too could not help but feel the strength of Manko's calling; the crowd which had gathered about was much larger than he had ever been able to draw, and he hated Manko for this too, knowing that he could not say so outright.

"This is my place!" he barked out at Manko in his frustration.

"We have only one place, brother," replied Manko solemnly, "and that place is in the bosom of the Lord." The congregation was quick to punctuate these words with, "Amen! Amen! Amen!"

"I say that you is a robber and a thief... You know damn well that this is my spot!" the preacher insisted, but Manko, still flat on the ground with the old man sitting on his chest, answered in Biblical phrases only. He had been completely humbled and humiliated and his voice was tinged with pathos, softened and lowered with resignation.

"The Lord said go out into the world and teach My holy word... I obey His commandments only," said Manko, to which the congregation added, "Amen! Amen! Amen!"

The old preacher looked swiftly from Manko to the crowd, then back at Manko. "So you obey His commandments only?" he asked with a wide leer across his face. He was filled with disgust and hate, yet he knew he was walking a tightrope, for he sensed the temper of the crowd, and he knew that they were on Manko's side. Now it was time to change that temper to his own favour.

"And what about his commandment that says, 'Thou shalt not steal'... eh? ...You forget that one?" he swept his arm through the air and brought down a crashing blow with the back of his hand upon Manko's face.

The crowd had grown so large now that people stood on milk boxes at the back to get a glimpse of what was going on; perched on nearby trees were children who could not get close enough to the preacher. At first no-one wished to interfere, they felt that this was an affair between two men of God, but slowly they had come to the conclusion that there was only one man of God, and that was the younger man. The old man was a crook, and when he struck Manko this time, it was enough.

"Why you aint behave yourself? You aint have no shame or what?" a short burly man called out to the preacher. It was more than a question, it was a statement, a command, and a threat; it meant that if the old preacher did not behave himself, the man would do something about it. The old preacher still sat on Manko's chest looking about the crowd. They had been shouting their disapproval, but when he looked up no one had really challenged him. This time, however, the short little man with stocky arms stepped forward. His arms and his chest were thick and powerful; they seemed out of proportion with the rest of his body, as though he had worked all his life with the top of his body and the muscles of his shoulders and arms stood out in lumps. The old preacher looked him up and down, then he sucked his teeth and dismissed him

"Who you talkin' to so rough?" he demanded. He could put people down with just the tone of his voice when he spoke to them that way.

"I talkin' to you!" the man insisted, coming closer to the preacher, his index finger jerking back and forth as he repeated, "You... you... you... you!"

The crowd sensed that it had a spokesman now, and they began shouting encouragement to the man. "Knock him down, man... Give him a good lick in he head... Mash 'im up, boy... go on... teach him a lesson... the bogus scamp."

There were others in the crowd who had not made up their minds as yet; they waited to see what would happen. A woman who was standing next to the man was among them.

"John-John," she cried out, "why you don't mind you own business and leave them two preachers alone?" John-John turned, not to her, but to the whole crowd.

"It aint have no two preachers here... it have one... and only one. An' this... this...," he snatched the old man by the scruff of his robes and drove his elbow with all his power hard into his stomach. "This crook aint have no shame. That is number one for the first blow you give this poor man while he have a Bible in he hand that you aint have no respect for." Then coming down with his thick fist upon the neck of the old preacher, "...And that is number two... If you want more, it have plenty more where that came from."

The old preacher looked up, rubbing his neck. He looked at the crowd which burst into peals of laughter, and he ran swiftly and disappeared into the sugar canes at the edges of the junction.

The congregation helped Manko up, and dusted off his robes. Someone handed him his Bible and the short man who'd knocked down the old preacher placed the parrot on Manko's shoulder. Everyone's voice was lowered and filled with respect when they addressed Manko, and he too, still feeling the pain of the blows he'd received, spoke in a voice that was humbled and hushed as he ambled away from the junction. When he got to his home, he felt his wounds one by one, going over them in great detail, recreating the scene and the blows, suffering through all his humiliation again and again with a kind of self-pity that both delighted and fascinated him. His heart was swollen; he felt choked and close to tears and in these moments felt that God was closest to him. This evening had convinced him, as he never was before, that he was called into the service of God.

Now, he thought, was the time to move into the heart of Port of Spain. He had been to the city on a few occasions and it had fascinated him; he remembered how his heart tumbled faster and quicker. There were more people, more rumshops, tramcars, bicycles and cars. The streets were overflowing with people, and he remembered how he had been carried along on its tide of bustle: that was enough.

Next morning he got on a bus on the Eastern Main Road, and headed for Port of Spain. The sun was up since six, and the roads were already hot. He could feel the pleasant warmth of the sun as his arm hung out the window of the bus, and since it was the hour when the city workers were on their way to their jobs, the bus was crowded. Manko could smell the people; a warm animal smell drifted back to him, and he looked at the faces, listened to the fragments of conversation, watched the countryside going past. He was filled with joy; a mild gurgling and churning spread from his stomach. He felt as though he was carrying out a plan that was ordained, something that had been planned over a number of years and was now coming into being with precision.

The bus came in along Marine Square, and the city was milling with workers at that hour. Manko felt the pulse and excitement of its noise and rush. He always felt this way about the city, as though something great and wonderful had taken hold of him, and he loved to let it carry him along on its tide, through the unknown streets, to new and different scenes and places. Today, however, he would not be able to enjoy that freedom. He had heard about a room in Frederick Street and he was going to rent it. He followed the street beyond shops and stores and came to a large tunnelled gateway whose great wooden doors were broken and stood against the walls of the dark passageway. From the street he could see a standpipe in the middle of the yard beyond, numbers of boulders heaped up together with clothes spread out on them to bleach in the sunlight, and a high wall of about ten feet at the back of the yard separating it from the yard in the next street. He went into a small shop at the side of the gate and the shopkeeper gave him two keys to the room in the yard, telling him that it was four-fifty a month, that he could take it or leave it, there would be no haggling over the price, because his mind was made up and he could get four-fifty for the room easily

The yard was flanked on either side by small rooms known as barracks, and at the side of each barrack room was a jumble of cooking utensils, stoves, charcoal braziers, and little supplies of charcoal on the ground. In front of some of the rooms were small chicken coops where the roomers kept a laying hen, or simply used them to lock up their fowls to prevent them from being stolen. Manko looked at the wall at the back of the yard and thought it was high enough to keep thieves from scaling it from the other side and making off with people's possessions, more particularly his own possessions, like his parrot who loved to be put out in the sun to repeat all the words he heard. No, not Lorrito, he could not bear the thought of some thief making off with his sole companion. But it was a good safe yard, and a nice room which remained in cool shade in the morning and got the last rays of the sun in the evening, and since Manko loved to sleep far into the mornings, he could not stand to have a room where the blatant morning sun came pelting its hot lashes at him, waking him up before his mind and body was ready to become attuned, slowly, deliciously, to the world about him.

The doors of the room bellied out on their loose hinges. They were held together by a small padlock whose leaf and tongue could be pried out with a screwdriver, but the feel of the key in his hand gave Manko a feeling of safeness and security. He opened the doors and they all but fell on him; he had to lift them up individually and scrape them through their arc, then place a boulder in front of each to prevent them from swinging shut. The room was empty except for a few pieces of old newspapers and some empty tin cans which the previous tenant had left behind. There was nothing more to see; it was still in half-darkness, and he closed the doors, snapping the padlock securely. It was his already, and he tried the key in the lock once or twice. When he saw a woman, the tenant next door, rattling her pots and pans as she started to make her breakfast, Manko was so pleased with everything he wanted to make friends right away.

"Morning, neighbour!" he greeted the woman who moved about half-asleep. She was dressed in a turquoise kimono, and down its back was a long oriental dragon stitched out in many colours. The woman was stooping down and he could see the clean contours of her body, unbroken by lines of underclothes against the tight smooth satin that hugged her body at each curve and undulation. She looked at him, squinting her eyes, then shook her head as though she had been dreaming, had woken suddenly and the image was gone, then she went back to lighting her stove again. She did not have a charcoal brazier like those standing in front of the other barracks, hers was a gleaming white two-burner kerosene stove; she had simply to put a match to it and she could put on her coffee.

"Morning, neighbour!" Manko repeated, and the woman looked up at him from her stooping position, her eyes squinting with disbelief and incredulity.

"You talkin' to me, Mister?" she asked, looking at him squarely this time as she noticed his robes. Manko looked about foolishly although he knew that there was no one else about and that she must certainly know that he was saying 'morning' to her.

"I only want to say good mornin'... that's all."

"Well, if is only good mornin' you want to say, you done say it already. I look as if I is your neighbour?"

Manko smiled sheepishly and walked out of the yard. As he walked away he heard her say, "Hm! Some people damn well fast in the world today. Neighbour, eh!"

By early nightfall, Manko was moved in. His chair, his cot, his table with the Bible on it had all found a place in the room, and everything looked as though they were that way for a long, long time. He met a few people in the yard as he was moving in and, noticing how they stared at his growth of hair and his full beard, he told them that he was a messenger of the Lord. They welcomed him with an awe and reverence that was touching, and this pleased him. There were a few children in the yard and they too lowered their voices when their parents told them to say 'evening' to the preacher. He let them come into his room and ogle the parrot. Lorrito was more excited than Manko with the change of place, the new air, the different room; and when the bird saw all the children it began to hurl fragments of biblical phrases at them. Manko then gave the bird its cue from *Ecclesiastes,* "To every thing there is a season, and a time to every purpose under heaven". The bird awaited its moment, and the children stood in silent respect, then Lorrito added, "A time to be born, and a time to die." Between Manko and the bird, they finished the lines with the children of the yard looking on at them as though they were both equally called into the service of the Lord.

The buildings in the yard on the other side of the wall were not high enough to be seen, but one could see the small hills that rose in the distance, and after the short glow of morning light coming from behind them, the sun burst through and began lashing the city with its whip-strokes. Its heat and its white light were enough to waken the yard, and people began rattling their pots and pans as they prepared dried codfish and bread, or threw smoked herrings into the embers of their braziers to roast. Children were jumping up and down with tin cups beside the single standpipe from which they caught water and poured it over their naked bodies, shrieking and screaming as the water struck their skin. Manko heard the yard awakening, but he still felt sleepy and pulled the pillow over his head to cover up the noise and din.

The yard emptied by eight o'clock. Most of its residents had left for work, and the children were off to school. Manko awoke half asleep, fed a banana to the parrot, then lay down in bed again to savour his awakening on the first day in the city. He could hear a faint rumble and low noise in the air, nothing like the drone of time in the quiet of the country and the sugar-estate town he came from, but a hum which held great possibilities of variety and adventure. All those lives moving about outside in the city filled him with curiosity and a feeling that something delightful was close and beckoning. His heart beat faster, his armpits sweated in thin, long drops that ran down his sides, and he could no longer lie in bed a mere listener, he wanted to become immersed in that hum and bustle of Port of Spain. As he washed and dressed late that morning, he felt excited and impatient to get out of the yard and mingle with the people in the streets, to see all the different faces of the city. He found himself brushing his teeth quickly and haphazardly; he rushed about and got dressed as though he had an appointment to keep with someone, and he was even impatient with Lorrito who seemed to be playing with the banana rather than eating it, and when he finally snapped the lock shut on the door he felt relieved. He looked at the woman's door next to his and saw that it too was locked, then he was out on the sidewalk of Frederick Street watching the cars and bicycles go past.

The streets were bustling with all the city people on their way to work, and Manko became instantly attuned to their rush and hurry; he too hurried along. The sidewalks were occasionally impassable where small cliques of workers stopped to chat and laugh with their comrades before going into their respective shops or stores, and he stepped off the curb to get past. Each time he did so, he felt a sense of joy and pleasure, as though he had done someone a good turn. He walked through streets without knowing them by name, stopped to look into shop windows, and time went past without his noticing. The streets were suddenly empty; it was that hour when all the clerks had arrived at their jobs and desks, and the other people, the shoppers, the housewives, the buyers had not arrived as yet. Although Manko was accustomed to being solitary, he began feeling that he was alone, that he knew no one, that no one would speak to him. It was close to ten o'clock, and the sun was lashing the awnings and the sidewalks with its white heat, and he pushed through the swinging doors of a rumshop, *The Prince of Wales Bar.* It was cool and quiet in the bar, its light was dimmed and he felt enveloped by the aromas of rum and bitters and fresh limes, and the sawdust sprinklings on the floor. He listened to the conversations of the people in the bar, but no one spoke to him until the bar attender came up and asked him for his order. He remembered what the old preacher had said about drinking rum, and he was about to order a bitters and soda, but was annoyed at himself and his own thoughts. Why should he have to listen to the prescriptions of that old faker? He was a man of God in his own right now, and if he wanted a rum, he wanted a rum. "A nip of Black Cat rum," he ordered the barman.

The habitues were scattered about in small cliques of five or six men drinking and talking. Each little knot of men was different. There were those who nestled in a corner and spoke in whispers, looking up with furtive looks as someone entered the bar, and they looked especially long at Manko, for he was a stranger. There were men who were afraid of the sun and its brash light, and there were those who stood close to the swinging doors so that they could see the street and whistle at the girls going past, then discuss the sizes of their legs and hips. And standing behind a tall tank of ice water on the counter was Manko's neighbour, the woman who lived next door. She was talking to two men, and Manko knew from the way they took turns looking at him that she had said something to them about him; and now they let out a great peal of laughter and guffaws, one of the men running the palm of his hand along the arcs and curves of her body, as if to accentuate them, in the way a bone is held before a dog and moved away each time the dog makes a bite for it. They laughed again when they saw that Manko understood their taunting. He heard the woman use the word 'preacher', then laugh in a high-pitched cackle, bringing her palm to her mouth as if to stop her own laughter, and as the cackle tumbled and jerked out of her throat, her slim whiplike body undulated and writhed until she was stooping, grasping the edge of the counter for support, her great round rolling eyes at the level of the counter staring at Manko.

At first he wanted to ask the three of them simply and quietly, now he wanted to shout his question at them: "You think that it is woman I want?... I is a man of God!" He was going to finish his rum and bring his glass crashing down upon the counter loud enough for them to hear, and see, and feel his anger, and the idea played across his mind with all its sound effects and gestures, and he imagined the way they would look across at him, startled and frightened. But as he played out the scene in his mind, the trio finished their drinks and started out of the rumshop laughing and staggering like three drunken sailors, each too drunk to walk by himself, arms locked about each other's waist. The woman was in the middle, and in that instant as they left the rumshop, Manko saw one of the men's hands slide up and squeeze the nipple of her breast.

*Miss Violet hail from a place call Cayacoo. If Trinidad is a small place, a small island sixty by forty miles, Cayacoo mus' be bout ten miles long and two miles wide. Now everybody have some kind of ambition in this world, and even people in the Caribbean want to better they position. So Miss Violet leave Cayacoo and she go to the New York City of the Caribbean, Port of Spain, Trinidad. A lotta people have a lotta t'ings in common but they don't even recognize it. The preacher couldn't find a damn t'ing to do wid heself in Trinidad, he couldn' find any kinda work and remember how he try to sweep out the doctor office believin that the doctor would teach him how to operate on people, how to give them injections, how to give them enema, how to make them feel good. Miss Violet want to do somet'ing wid she life too. She wasn't too different from the preacher. But if you meet a man who say that he have an ambition, rightaway you would say, well, that fella have a good head on he shoulders; if you meet a woman who say she want to make somet'ing of sheself, who go say she have a good head on she shoulders? Now that is we business here, to ax why people have ambition, o' why man have ambition and woman have ambition and both of them different. If you ax a man how he different from a woman, he could tell you rightaway.*

*Miss Violet was a special kinda girl, who use to like to have a man, and it start very early in she life. The first time she had a man, she was twelve years old in Cayacoo. The way it happen was that they use to have all kinda big sugar estate, and they use to have all kinda big-house, all kinda mansion that the white people use to live in. And then when they went away, all of them big houses was sittin' aroun' and then they was fallin' apart, and Miss Violet uses to go to one of them houses, and she use to dance and she use to sing. Now, she dance and she sing and she had the idea of what all o' them white people, when they was there, use to look like, how they use to get dress-up and how they use to have long skirt, long dress, and how all of the white man and them use to dress up wid bow-tie and scissors-tail jacket and that is the kinda old house that Miss Violet use to play and sing and dance in when she was twelve years old.*

*One day when she was singin' and dancin' a man come up in the house and he see she and he start to dance with she and he hold she and play with she breasts and he touch she spine and Miss Violet didn't know what she was feelin. The man stretch she out on the floor and Miss Violet would be the first one to tell you that she like it. She never see the man again, but she learn somet'ing from that man. She learn that she enjoy somet'ing what happen and she learn that she want more of that somet'ing, and if that is the kinda t'ing that make Miss Violet end up the way she end up, well, learning is learning, and if you meet anybody in the Caribbean tomorrow; the first t'ing he would tell you is that one of the most important t'ing in the world is to learn. Miss Violet want to have more and more of that learning, and it have a certain kinda learning that some people like and they say, "That is a good t'ing." If you learn how to be a mechanic, that is a good t'ing. If you learn how to be a doctor or a lawyer or a dentist, that is a good t'ing. But it have a different kinda t'ing when you learn what Miss Violet learn. People look at you and say, "You is a damn idler, you is a whore, you is a common prostitute." So Miss Violet was what? She wasn't born that way, she didn't ax to be that way. Somet'ing happen to she that day and that is what she want to have more and more of. She never t'ink for one moment that all o' the fellas who use to come into the yard and make love to she was comin' in and takin' somet'ing from she. But understan' how she have a certain kinda scruple. She say that although a hundred, five hundred men come in and make love to she, that if somebody peep at she, well, that was a different t'ing. If somebody come up to she and say, 'You not tryin' to make anybody happy, you just like to make money and you is a woman and you find a way to make money; if somebody come up to she and say, "All you does do is lie down there and let one man after another come in, look at you, come inside of you"; if somebody was to say that Miss Violet hate what she was doing, well, people like to say all kinda t'ings. Miss Violet enjoy life, she enjoy cooking she stew, she enjoy men. She didn't t'ink it was a bad t'ing to enjoy men, to have a lotto men.*

*Now somet'ing very funny does happen when ambition go in a certain direction. Because Miss Violet have a lot o' ambition. She didn't go to look for a job in the airlines, she didn't go to look for a job in the Government Treasury, she didn't go to look for a job working for the Trinidad Guardian, she didn't go for a job selling clothes in a department store. No. That might be the kinda t'ing that make a lotta women turn into whores in a lotta different, different places in the world. That very first day when she was only twelve years old and she was layin' on the floor of this old-time falling-down house where the planks was falling apart, where the trees and the bush was growin' up aroun' the house, and where she use to go and she use to dance by sheself and when the man come up and he start to dance with she, Miss Violet like all o' dat. Miss Violet remember how she could see the remnants of one of the old-time chandeliers with all kinda glass that look like a lotta pieces of bottle, break-up bottle, Miss Violet like that. Miss Violet remember how the light comin' in t'rough the window look on the man back. Miss Violet look at sheself, she look at she body and she like the way it look and Miss Violet, even afterwards, when the man finish up and he run away and she went back home and she look at sheself in the mirror, she see somebody else. And she like that. She like the way she face look, she like the way she eyes look. She want to put on lipstick and she want to put on rouge, and she want to put on somet'ing that would make she body look even more powerful than it lookin' already.*

*The man jus' come into the house and he ax she, "You want to dance with me?" and she say, "Yes." She never t'ink for one moment that the man goin' to hurt she. She was dancin', she was hearin' music, she was seein' all o' the old-time days, she was seein'' all o' the people who use to live in that house, and she did hear a lotta stories bout how people use to live in them days. Them was the old-time days, them was the days that belong to somebody else. Them was the days that people who don't have no kinda memory have, they have only a memory o' somebody else memory.*

*But we mustn't stand still too long. We mus' always keep moving. We mus' always go from here to there and somebody tell we that is a good t'ing. To repeat, if man say that he want to be the greates' dentist in the world, everybody would say, "Dat's a damn good t'ing, boy." If a woman" well that is somet'ing else, that is another story.*

*So Miss Violet was a little whore; she had a body that help she along the way. Miss Violet had the breasts and the nipples, the hips and the waist. Miss Violet had all the necessary equipment.*

Anger was still coursing through his body when Manko left the bar, but he could feel it subsiding slowly, and he forced his mind to dwell upon other things. He began by telling himself that if he had had his robes on they would have had a little more respect for him, then he immediately saw that if he was in his robes, carrying about his great Bible, he would not dare go into a rumshop. Each thought of revenge was immediately countered and discredited in his own mind, and he felt pushed and oppressed by two great grinding stones with him in the middle as they made grist of him. His first sally into the city so depressed him he began thinking how short life was; it consisted of one moment, and that was at the junction when God acknowledged him in the eyes of the people. Manko felt his life short because time which is endless and infinite amounted to only seconds for him. He had no memory to speak of, no days of joy or great emotion which he could call upon to lengthen his past. Like the monotony of the rainy season, the boredom of pelting sun, so was his life. And if he sought anything at all, it was to efface this silencing monotony that haunted him; he wished to fill in the empty holes of what time he had left so that his life would seem long, meaningful and important, so that somewhere along its invisible, linear path he could feel that he was a part of it, that it had not dismissed him without at least winking at him for a single moment, however short.

As he moved through the streets, he began to feel tired; he had gone through some streets twice without knowing it, and then towards afternoon he crossed a bridge which looked down a deep gorge. Beyond, the hills which encircle the city began their rise, and standing on one of the small mounds was a large cross of gold shining in the light of the afternoon sun. The sight of it made Manko feel better; he was no longer winded and tired. He inquired of a passer-by on the bridge how to get to the cross, and started off in that direction.

The mound was traced by a zigizag cobblestone path that wove back and forth, and at each turn of the path was a stone pillar about six feet high containing a recessed plaque of sculptured bronze. Each one depicted one of the twelve stations of Christ on his way to Calvary. The mound was in fact called Calvary Hill, and Manko studied each of the bronze depictions on his way to the top of the hill where he could see some workmen sitting about at the foot of the cross eating and chatting. They looked up anxiously and pretended to be busy at work, but when Manko got close to them, they stopped work and began loafing again.

The top of the mound was a small flat terrace, rimmed by a low cement wall, and at one end was a small chapel facing the cross. At the foot of the cross lay a life-sized image of Christ crucified that the workmen had taken down from the cross. The men were still working on the image, their little pots of colours and paint brushes scattered around. They had already done the holes in the hands and feet, the deep incision in the breast, and the drops of blood that fell from the crown of thorns. One of the men got up and stretched. His body quivered as he stood on his tiptoes and yawned with a loud, deep sigh. "Oh, Lawdee Lawd," he said, stretching his arms and his torso, his eyes closed and his mouth a dark hole, and then opening his eyes and seeing the image of Christ, he said, "Man! You look as if you really in agony! Why the hell you didn't mind your own business?"

The words nettled Manko, and he wanted to say something, but the men had ignored him as he sat on the edge pretending to look over the city.

"How about a couple of quick rolls?" the man asked his fellow workers, and they all scampered up as he seated himself on the chest of the statue and began rattling a pair of dice. He cupped his hands, blew into them, then sent the dice rolling. There was laughter, shouting, swearing, and a few obscenities. Manko looked with pain at the flattened abdomen, and the fragile rib-cage of the Lord, on which the workman sat, and all the agony on the face of Christ seemed born out of the ugly and grotesque scenes which were being acted out here and now. The thought raced across his mind that he should jump up onto the empty pedestal of the cross, stretch his arms wide and say aloud to the gamblers, "Come and crucify me once more..." One of the men whispered something, then they all scurried about and squatted down beside their little pots of colour and began painting the image diligently as the sound of footsteps got closer.

"You boys working hard?" a man, whom Manko assumed was their foreman, asked as he came onto the terrace, and they all answered, "Yes, chief... Sure, chief... Look at how much we have finished, chief!" Manko was still angry, and he wished to complain, to punish; he desired revenge for a hurt that remained unclear in his mind. He had taken insult and abuse before, turning the other cheek, but now God had called him, and if he was angered, it was God's wish, and God's way of directing him. The thought was a frightening one, but the strength and power it gave Manko to seek God's revenge was exciting. He got up and went over to the foreman and told him what wastrels the workmen were. He complained about their idleness while he was away, and then turned directly to the workmen and began berating them.

"You have no shame! You gamble, you spit, you curse, and you sit on the chest of the Lord God Jesus Christ... and you," he spoke to the man who had addressed the bust, "You mock the agony of the Lord... Who do you think he died to save?" Some of the men held their heads low in silence, others tried to continue painting, but no one dared look Manko in the face and even the foreman was silent. No one knew who Manko was; what if he were one of the clerics of the chapel and reported the whole story to its head? They listened to him speechless, and when they did not answer, he forced on his advantage. "Eh?" he insisted, bending over the workman who had asked Jesus why he hadn't minded his own business.

The foreman gestured to the workman to stand up when he spoke to the preacher and he rose slowly to face him. "Repent!" Manko shouted at him. The man looked foolishly to his comrades, then to his foreman, then to Manko. "How you mean repent?" he inquired sheepishly.

"How I mean repent? How I mean repent?" asked Manko, his voice high-pitched and angry as he grasped the man by the neck of his collar, dragged him close to the bust, and forced him down on his knees. "Now repeat after me: Holy Father."

The workman repeated solemnly after Manko, "Holy Father."

"Forgive me."

"Forgive me."

"For I am a sinner."

"Ignorant of Thy ways."

"Ignorant of Thy ways."

"Ignorant of Thy Presence."

"Ignorant of Thy Presence."

"Which is everywhere."

"Which is everywhere."

"I have sinned and blasphemed before Thee."

"I have sinned and blasphemed before Thee."

"And I ask Thy forgiveness."

"And I ask Thy forgiveness."

"Amen."

"Amen."

"Now get up, you damned rogue!"

The foreman tipped his hat to Manko, thanking him, as the workmen lifted up the bust and carried it into the chapel facing the empty cross. He looked at the vertical and the horizontal of the cross, and it seemed empty without the image of Christ on it. He wondered how long it would take the workmen to finish repainting the image and mount it back on the cross. He lingered on the terrace looking out over the city, thinking of all the men and women who must be looking in this direction and seeing the empty cross glistening in the sun. Then he walked down the mound and set out for home.

As he entered his gateway he smelt the aromas of a wonderful stew. He could trace the thyme and the onions, the chives and the garlic, all mixed in with burnt brown sugar and butter and he was preparing to make some compliment to the cook, but when he saw that it was the woman next door, he only smiled. He wished he could say something to her like, "Neighbour, why don't we start out from the beginning...?" She stood in her kimono, one hand on her hip, the other holding her pot spoon like a weapon she would use to defend herself with if attacked. Manko lowered his eyes as he passed her, and as he worked his key in the padlock, be heard her grunt, "Hm!" He turned to see her bent over at the waist, the lid in one hand as she smelt the stew. "The pleasures of the flesh too strong... too strong for people with weak stomach," she said. Manko watched her hips and her shoulders swivel on the pivot of her navel as she stirred the stew, and the evening sunlight, coming in horizontal shafts from the hills beyond, cast sheens of light and shadow under her breast and up along the inside walls of her thighs as her body worked, naked under the green satin of her kimono.

"You talkin' to me, neighbour?" Manko inquired. He felt foolish as soon as the words left his lips, and she looked him up and down as before in a few seconds of intense silence before she let her anger fly.

"I don't want no preacher livin' next to me, following me all over the place, spying on me... peeping at my business through the holes in the wall at all hours of the night." Some of the other tenants in the yard heard the commotion and the high pitched voice of anger and they just stood outside their doors to listen.

It was sheer accident that Manko's sleeping and waking habits coincided with hers; he too loved the night, and sat up late until after the yard was still and empty. Sometimes he read his Bible, other times he just sat waiting for night to come and enfold him; and it happened more than once that the woman next door came home late and saw him sitting in his chair with his Bible in his lap. Pretending to read while he was really spying on her, she thought.

"You waiting up for me? Or you waiting for God?" she asked him. Manko ignored her. Her words nettled him, but he closed his Bible and went into his room without answering her.

Next morning he was awakened by the sound of hammering. He turned over in his bed and lay there listening to the woman's voice as she pounded away. She got several discs cut off from the tops of tin cans and went about nailing them over tiny holes and crevices in the partition between her room and Manko's, and with each stroke of the hammer he could hear her angry voice.

"Always (bang) peeping!... (bang) Peeping (bang), peeping (bang), peeping (bang). He playing preacher, but he peeping at my business... day and night... night and day. I can't have no privacy in my own house. Let me see how he go peep at me now."

The hammering stopped and Manko began to stir about. He could still hear her grumbling about in the yard, then she came back into the room and started hammering all over again. She had run out of tin discs, and now she took some old newspapers, twisted lengths of them into tight, long ropes, and hammered them into the remaining crevices. When she was finished, she drew a long breath and shouted loud enough so that Manko could hear her. "Peep at me one more time and see if I aint go down to Police Headquarters and report you... Playing preacher, huh!"

Manko went to Calvary Hill where he spent the day examining each engraved station of Christ carrying the cross and then he spent a long while admiring the empty golden cross at the top of the hill before he went back to his room.

Darkness fell quickly in the city, and with it came peacefulness and quiet. The neighbours called in their children who were playing in the yard, and from the doorways of the barracks there were only shafts of pale light and voices tuned down to low grumbling and whispering. Manko drew his chair out into the yard where he could look up to the stars, and if an occasional late-corner went past, he called out, 'evening', and the preacher answered, 'evening', to that unknown voice. The yard was friendly that way and Manko felt taken into its world and its ways. The woman next door was not in, and Manko began thinking of her again. He thought of all the ways he would approach her, with friendliness and warmth. Now that he was indeed her next door neighbour, perhaps she would feel differently about him. Perhaps he was fast and forward, calling her neighbour when he had just looked over the room. He was after all a complete stranger to her, and she had every right to protect herself.

He could hear the hour and half-hour and quarter hour rings of the Trinity Church as he waited in the darkness of the yard, and after several rings, he began feeling that the night was long. Time had slipped past so smoothly before. His mind played with nothing and everything, and days, weeks, months went past, but now he became uncomfortable and he moved back and forth on his chair when the woman did not appear, and when he heard twelve o' clock ring, he decided to go indoors and go to sleep, but he only tossed about. His limbs felt tight and drawn, and he stretched them as far as they would go with long deep sighs of relief. He called out to the parrot in the dark, but the bird replied only with a sleepy caw and Manko himself finally dropped off to sleep again. In the remaining hours of that morning's sleep, he had a horrifying dream. He dreamt that his ears were cut off, and he held them, one in each of his hands like the open Bible, staring at them. The dream was painless and soundless, and with a feeling that was more sorrow than pity, he tried to replace his ears, knowing deep within himself that it was futile, that his ears once removed would never root themselves to his head again.

As he washed and bathed that morning, the details of his dream appeared as if out of nowhere, and Manko tried to push them out of his mind. He could see the cross up on the hill from his yard, and he turned his attention to the cross in an attempt to forget the dream. Later on he journeyed to the top of the hill and sat under the cross for hours. He envisioned the small enclosure packed with people listening to his sermons. But something always stood in his way, some inner thought would cross his mind. "Suppose I forget the lines from the Bible?" he would ask himself, and then trying to recite one of the psalms which he knew by heart, he would indeed find that he had forgotten a line or two and had to go back to the Bible to check them. He was doing just this when a policeman entered the yard, and as he emerged from the dark tunnel of the gateway, Manko saw that he was accompanied by the woman next door. Deep into the night Manko had heard the sounds of footsteps and sometimes they must have been the sounds of the same hobnailed boots that he heard now as the two entered the yard. The woman had brought any number of men into the yard late at night; it was no secret to the other yard dwellers, but they respected her discretion and they treated her with the courtesy and respect they held for all the other residents; there were indeed those who held her in awe and sometimes fear. She could coax the shopkeeper to give someone credit with a little of her coquetry, or she could get one of the street vendors to give fruits to the little children in the yard simply by pinching his cheek and screwing up her lips in the form of a kiss, and when one of the men in the yard got arrested one night for riding a bicycle without a light, she managed to get the case dropped before it got to the magistrate.

Manko sat in his chair reading the Bible and when he saw the two he dropped his eyes, for he was surprised that she should bring one of her men friends into the yard in broad daylight. And then the policeman was standing directly in front of him.

"Your name is Manko... the preacher?" He looked up and saw the policeman holding a blue summons in his hand.

"That's right," Manko answered. Meantime the woman had gone into her room, and he could hear her high-pitched laughter.

"I have a summons here for you to appear in the Magistrate's Court for peeping at people." As the policeman pronounced these words, there was a loud cackle of laughter from the woman's room again.

"You know how to read?" the policeman asked. "I have to know that you understand what this summons mean, otherwise we have to get somebody to explain it to you in my presence."

Manko was nettled. "Read **and** write," he said sharply.

"That good," the policeman said, handing him the blue summons and leaving the yard; then the woman began singing: "Gentle Jesus, meek and mild."

If she gave herself to anyone, she thought, if she sold her body to anyone, that was one thing, but this was something else. She felt used as an image or a photograph or a film or a face in an advertisement was used by people she did not know or care about, and that image evoked all forms of lust or passion or hungering which she resented. She could not be persuaded that the lust or passion stirred up in a man had something to do with him and his dark mind. She saw herself as the source of that stolen pleasure; even if her body was not even touched by anyone, she resented any pleasure they might get without consent.

Manko sat in his chair reading the summons as she sang on. She was the complainant, he read, she had spent five shillings to get him charged with peeping at her, and he had to appear in court in a week. The summons had a strange effect on him, it shook him from a sleep that had overtaken him, and now he began rustling about. He decided that he would go to Calvary Hill and preach that very day, and towards dusk, he stood beneath the tall golden cross with his Bible in his hand reading and then interpreting freely in his rich warm tones. Then as anger shot through him, his voice became harsh and he bellowed out his cries until they re-echoed within the small enclosure of the summit. An occasional passer-by making a short cut to his home stopped for a moment and looked the preacher up and down, then went on his way. Manko had washed and bathed and was dressed in his long white robes, his beard was now full and he looked like an ancient shepherd of biblical times as he railed against sin, rum-drinking, chicken-stealing and cursing. The evening was still light, and although few people stopped to listen, he felt that others were still due from their jobs down in the city. There were about five people who gathered about him out of curiosity. Some had stood out of reverence, or a kind of shame, because they could not turn away from the words of God, much as they would have liked to go on home to their crab callalloo and rice. And Manko preached on, for the words and the sermons came as if by themselves. He found himself asking his brethren to love, to cast out hate, and within himself he felt such an intense hate for the woman in the yard that his sermon became rich and compelling. He preached on until the spirit which had moved him was spent. He did not care that his listeners had dwindled to three by the end; he felt warm and exhilarated, and when he looked down on the offering cloth, no one had left a single penny.

He felt depressed and dejected as he walked back home to the yard. Was it the money? Was it because no one cared enough to leave some small offering to God? He never cared for money, why should he now? He would push the thought out of his mind. Had he not been called? Had God not spoken to him? He recalled all the signs he had asked for, how God had spoken with the black and white horse in the evening, with fires in the cane fields, with the lizard skittering across the floor, and finally with the falling mango leaf. He would push it out of his mind, he would stop off somewhere and get a rum. As he thought of this, he discovered that he was near to the Prince of Wales Bar. He recalled that the woman next door had been there before, and he became curious and anxious as he approached the bar. He could easily go somewhere else, but no, now it became urgent and imperative that he should go to the Prince of Wales Bar. Where he was tired before, his body felt suddenly shot through by a great heat, and his limbs moved smoothly, his pace changed, and the image of the woman standing in the kimono came back to him. He could see the arcs and curves of her breasts and her belly as she stood silhouetted in the sunlight that morning.

He could hear the sounds of laughter and the hum of conversation before he entered the bar; there were still those who hung about before going home when the rumshops closed at eight o'clock. As he entered the bar, his body quivered with the odours of rum, and the old casks and puncheons which never left the place. The bar attender came over and took Manko's order in lowered tones, tones of respect, and tones of reluctance. He did not particularly like to have preachers in the Prince of Wales, he did not like to have people start preaching God in his bar; there was sure to be trouble.

"You sure you don't want to take it out?" he asked Manko as he stood for a second or two hoping that the preacher would change his mind, and do his drinking somewhere else. On the other hand it pleased Manko. Before, he could go into a rumshop and no-one would care. No one saw him come and go, and if he died quietly somewhere, no-one would miss him in the rumshop. Now he was a man of God, and there was always some notice of him; he presented a picture to people, they had to think twice about him; even here in the rumshop, they had to look at him and take him into account; he was no longer just another man buying a nip of rum.

"What wrong with my money? It have hole in it or what?" Manko challenged the bar attender. "I come in here and ask you for a nip just like everybody else; now make haste before I call a policeman." The bar attender shrugged his shoulders and went to get Manko's order, but when he returned, he did not place it in front of him, he set down the little tray with the rum and pitcher of ice water some yards away so that Manko would not be near to a clique of drinkers who stood close by, and he motioned Manko over with a flick of his thumb. Manko picked up his Bible and the parrot squawked as they moved to the far end of the counter. It was darker here, and he could not see out into the street, and no one would go past, back and forth; it was like drinking by oneself; or taking the nip home and drinking it there, and that was not why you paid six cents more to drink the same rum in a rumshop. The bar attender came and stood in front of him with his arms stretched out along the counter waiting for his money as Manko uncorked the bottle and poured out the rum leisurely. The man still did not speak. "Let him wait," thought Manko. "If he don't want to talk up is he own business." Finally the bar attender began rubbing his thumb and index finger, asking Manko to pay up. Manko looked up at him with fake surprise, then he jerked his thumb to the spot where he had stood. The bar attender looked and saw that he had left the money there. He threw Manko a cutting glance as he picked up the money, then put it in the cash register and slammed it shut. Manko then heard the sound of laughter again; he looked across the bar and there was his next door neighbour drinking with three men. When she was certain that Manko had seen her, she rolled up the fingers of one hand, leaving a tiny aperture between them, then she placed her hand close to one of the men's eyes and began laughing out loud.

"You know how to peep?" she asked the man. "Peep through this peephole and tell me what you see." The four of them were in high spirits, and the men were going along with her whims, though not understanding why.

"Ah... I see... I see... ah..."

"Look harder," she ordered the man, and now her hand was placed so that it faced Manko.

"I see a man with a long, long beard and a long white robe," the man said finally, and they all burst into gales of drunken laughter, though no-one looked directly at Manko.

"You mean to tell me that you see a preacher?" the woman said, "Here in a rum shop? I can't believe it. Let me peep and see." She then looked at Manko through the slit between her fingers, though her eyes swept along the counter without pausing on him. "I must be getting blind, darling... I can't see nothing." The men insisted that there was a preacher, and she insisted that she saw no-one, but they all understood that something was hilariously funny, though the men did not know what.

Manko threw two large shots down his throat, then he put the cork in the mouth of the bottle and slapped it hard. The woman saw the anger in his gesture, and let out one of her high-pitched cackles as Manko slipped the half-filled nip of rum into a slitted pocket of his robe and stalked out of the rumshop.

When he got home, the yard was already in darkness. The parrot was half-asleep on his shoulder and he placed the bird on its perch for the night, then he drew out his chair into the yard and began reading his Bible. The words, the thoughts in the book, the peace and quiet of the yard and the night calmed him; he felt as though he could forgive anyone anything, and his heart felt full and physically enlarged in his bosom. After he had read for about an hour, he heard footsteps coming through the tunnelled gateway, and as the footsteps got closer and the figure finally emerged, he saw that it was his next door neighbour. This time he would find out just what made her dislike him. He was not only calm, but penitent, he was ready to forgive, but something else stirred in him. He saw himself naked, thought of himself with faults, he felt that there could be a great many things that were evil about him, perhaps he did not see himself as others did, and it was in this humbled tone that he spoke to the woman.

"Why you hate me so bad?" he asked her. The woman was startled when he spoke to her. They had passed each other in the yard on the way to the standpipe or the shower without even looking up at each other. "From the first day you see me you hate me," Manko went on, "You didn't even know me... you didn't even know me name when I first walk in the yard, and you hate me from that day."

She sensed the softness in his voice and she felt forced into becoming gentle and searching. Manko's tone caught her in a spell for a few seconds, but then the spell broke and she became filled with hate and rage. She was surprised herself at how suddenly her mood changed, perhaps it was the rum and that rush of the alcohol like an explosion that smashed at her brain.

"I didn't know you," she said, "but I could smell you. You see how you know one sermon pon another... by heart? Well, is the same with me. I don't know nothing bout Bible and sermon and sin, but I know bout **men.** It get so I could smell one from the other, and when I smell a rotten one, I know him."

Manko listened; it was the first time she spoke directly. Nothing would shake him from his tranquillity; he let her go on. Some of the yard dwellers poked their heads out of their doors to see what was going on, then they went back in without saying anything, while Manko sat in his chair nodding his head in assent each time the woman spoke. This annoyed her even more.

"You playing holy," she shouted, "but you like women... I know... and you like rum, and you always watching... you always watching people... It have something bad in your eyes. You think I don't know what goes on in you mind? Ha! I know your mind better than you, and I aint only know your mind, I see you with my own two eyes peeping at me. You know what I look like... you know what I look like underneath my clothes?" Manko was surprised by her question, he kept staring at her, and he found that somewhere in the darkness of his memory he knew what she looked like undressed. Was he sleepwalking... Did he peep at her one night without knowing it? Or did he imagine what her naked body looked like? He felt thrown up against a wall, pinned and defenceless, and all he could say to her was, "Thank you for those words neighbour... Good night."

"Thank you, eh," the woman repeated angrily, "Good night, eh? Wait till tomorrow morning; then we will hear what you have to tell the magistrate in the Court House. I hope they put you in jail and throw way the key!"

Manko lay sleepless in bed, thoughts turning over in his mind like old leaves. Just as he felt the pains or the anguish of the Lord, just as he felt joy and exaltation on reading a sermon, so he felt all the emotions of his thoughts just as though they were actually happening to him at the moment. He had never been to a Court House, yet he knew the feeling of dread, fear, and the embarrassment of being accused of peeping at a woman. How simple it was to have his life undone. He would not only be the laughing stock of people, they might chase him away, they might curse him, they might even stone him. He had been the one to ask people to admit their sins; he had asked them to repent. Tomorrow would be different; he himself would be judged, and someone else the judge.

And then too, the woman's voice came back to him again. "You know what I look like... you know what I look like underneath my clothes." He had seen her that first day when he came into the yard, bent over, stirring her pot, and her angular body moved under her kimono. He remembered thinking that she must not be wearing anything else underneath. He remembered the colour of the kimono; it was turquoise, with a high raised threaded design of an oriental serpent curled down the back, and as she bent over, she had caught the bottom of the kimono and tucked it between her thighs, and the bottom half of the serpent had curled up between her thighs. He remembered the dream he had when his ears dropped off, and now he suddenly remembered that there was more to the dream, that it had something to do with his neighbour, and it became clear to him that he had held her naked body in his arms in his dream. That was when he knew what she looked like; or did he get up during his dream and look through one of the holes in the wall? He searched his mind for a picture of her body, and it came easily; he found that he knew each curve and each undulation, each mound of her breast, waist, bottom; he knew her body. And as these images raced through his mind, he found it impossible to erase them, he found it impossible to find a posture on his bed which would bring on sleep.

The yard remained quiet except for an occasional dweller who had run out of water and went to the standpipe, and the night was punctuated only by the church bell at Trinity ringing out the quarters, halves and hours as they went past. He let out a deep groan of despair, and Lorrito began cawing. The bird moved to the end of the stick on which it was perched as though it wanted to get as far away from the wall as possible. When it was at the end of the perch, it began fluttering its wings as if to fly away. Its cawing now changed, and Manko could tell that something had frightened the bird. He got up and stretched out his finger which the bird climbed onto, and as he stroked the feathers on the bird's neck, he looked up at the perch where he saw two small shafts of light. Now they were visible, now they were gone, as though something moved on the other side of the wall. He was flooded with anger, and he swung his outstretched palm at the holes in the wall with all his strength. Then he felt the pain rush through his arm, and his palm felt cold from the blow. Then there was a loud crash next door, followed by sudden cries of pain as the woman fell from the chair on which she stood peeking at him. He jumped up on his bed and looked through the hole, and saw her lying on the floor rubbing her side; she was completely naked, looking up to the holes in the wall and, as though she knew that Manko must now be looking through the holes, she sprang to her feet and blew out the kerosene lamp with a loud swoosh.

Manko could no longer stand the stretching out of time. Night became a long dark season through which he waited. He no longer cared about the outcome of his case before the magistrate. What was more pressing now was time; he wished to get all of this behind him. He lay in bed still feeling the pain in the palm of his hand, and he could see the first dim rays of morning light coming through the openings in the doors. Then he heard someone grumbling outside in the yard. There were a few moments of silence followed by angry clattering and more swearing. He finally got up and opened his doors. At the far end of the yard in the last barrack room against the wall, lived the man with a pushcart. He was busy pulling things out, then pushing them back and forth in a frenzy.

"Morning neighbour... you lose something?" Manko asked. The man stopped his poking and searching like a thief caught in the act.

"No... no, everything alright," he told Manko, who shrugged his shoulders and went on to get washed and dressed.

*But everyt'ing wasn't so alright at all, not to say that the pushcart man like to lie, he was an honest man deep down in he heart, and he learn that lesson long long time gone. One of the worst t'ings to be in this worl' was a t'ief... He poopah and he moomah always tell he so from the time he was a chile, and he know that if you want somet'ing in the world, you have to work hard fo' it. If you see somebody else have somet'ing, it belongin' to them... is not yours.*

*The man come to live in the yard a long long time with he poopah and moomah. They did come from Tunapuna, one of them small village up in the country, and the family move to this same room where he livin' now. Time pass, t'ings change, and he poopah and moomah get fed up with livin' in Port of Spain and went back to the country and they little garden and cow and two three goat and chicken. The boy only have sixteen years, and when he see that it look like they can't afford to feed he and mind he, he had to leave school and find a work. But t'ings was so bad when the yankee dollar wasn't floatin' roun' no more, he was lucky to have a roof over he head, and he stop in that same room. He try to find a work, but nuttin' doin, everybody cryin' hard-up. All he seein' all over the town was all kinda sign that say 'no idlers', 'no liming'. The town turn upside down when the Yankees leave. People t'iefin' left and right; you can't leave a chicken outside in a coop in them days, otherwise it disappear and turn into chicken stew, or curry chicken, and them t'ief so smart, they bury the feathers and bone and everything, just to be on the safe side.*

*One day he was talkin' to a old man who had a pushcart, and the old man say he could give him a job if he want to help out. It was better than nuttin', so he take it. He was a damn hard worker and the old man couldn't do hard work no more, so he sell the cart to him.*

*He feel nice at first. He was he own boss, and he could keep he own hours. People from roun' the market know him from the time he work for the old man... they know he is a honest man. He live in Port of Spain waitin' for the day when he have nuff save up to go back to Tunapuna and buy a piece of lan' and make a small garden, but t'ings goin' up everyday: food, room rent, and after a time, it look like if he even forget bout the garden and Tunapuna... them t'ings was only a dream now. He could only get a nip of Black Cat rum sometimes and drink it in the evening and wonder where the ass he life gone to. He mus' be had twenty odd years, but he look like an old old man, and he feel like an old old man. Plenty people in the yard know him, and they respec' him because he was a quiet man and a hard workin' man, and he livin' in the yard longer than mos' other people. He had to take a few shillin' to he poopah and he moomah now and then, because he remember how much they did want he to get education... how hard they try till they had to take him out from school and put him to work.*

*It had a small hole in the wall where he poopah and moomah uses to hide the few shillings they had, and he use to hide he savin' in the same hole... put back two brick and close up the hole. This mornin' when he gone to look for he money... it gone! The man couldn't believe he own eye. He sit down on the step and he t'inkin' of the old time days, and how he moomah and poopah save they money in the same hole and nobody ever t'ief it. How t'ing does happen so at all? How a man does get old so quick? He start t'inkin of the days when they first come to live in this room, how he didn't know nobody, he was only a chile, and how he use to go to Woodford Square and play cricket whole evenin' till it get dark, and he remember before that time when he went to the square day in and day out, watchin' the other boys play cricket, 'til one day the boys come up to him.*

*"Aye... Thinny-Boney! You want to play?" one of the boys call out to him, and although he hear and he know they was callin' him, he keep pullin' out the red petals from a hibiscus flower, tearin' off the bottom ends and blowin' through the fine pores of needle holes at the bottom til the petals swell out like a thin pink balloon, then he take out a straight pin from he shirt and pierce a hole in the balloon.*

*"Matchstick foot! You playin' deaf? You want to play, or you don't want to play?"*

*In he own childish way, the boy understand that if he answer to any of the nickname that they call him, he go have to live with it for the rest of he life. It was two weeks now since they did move to Port of Spain, and he start to go to Woodford Square in the evenin'. At first he use to sit by the fountain with he thin long legs danglin' in the water, spray fallin' all over he face, and when nobody crossin' through the square, he walk cross the waist-high water to the green and mossy man-size bust. It had a giant of a man standing like some God on top of four half-fish half-woman creatures, a tall trident in he powerful arm pointin' to the shell of blue-blue sky. He touch the strong green veins runnin' down the calves of the man leg with fear, half expecting the severe lips to smile, or even curl up in anger at he; but the lips remain still and severe. Then he hold he cheek close to the small breast of one of the smilin' women who was sittin' back to back, and he t'ink that he see she smile.*

*"Aye... you! Wha-you name? You have a name or you aint have a name?"*

*He was lookin' at the boys through slitted eyes, still sittin' on the foot-high cement runner that run round Woodford Square with tall iron rail pierce deep in it. For the whole of the last week and the week before he use to come and sit on the runner to watch the boys play cricket 'til firefly come out in the square and the boys go home with they bat and wicket and ball, then he get up and catch firefly and put them in a small white phial to put under he pillow so that he could watch them glow in the dark when they blow out the kerosene lamp.*

*"Aye... no name... That is your name?"*

*"I name Bolan," he say with a sullen look in he eye as he watch the six or seven boys who stop the game and was standin' around from they battin' or bowlin' or fieldin' positions... waiting for him.*

*"Well... you want to play, or you don't want to play? Cat bite you tongue or what?"*

*His parents did leave they ajoupa hut in Tunapuna, and they lend they two cow to he uncle so that he father could work as a cutlass-man in the airbase the Yankee was buildin' in Chaguaramas, and the boy went to Market School in the back of Eastern Market where it have thousands of voices of the customers, vendors and live animals that come screamin' through the school window, so that he couldn't hear what the teacher was sayin' sometime. That cost six lashes in the palm for what the teacher say was day-dreamin. When he finally find out what day-dreamin mean, he feel like if the teacher cut deep inside of he and discover a secret that he keep from everybody else, because he mind use to really run away with him... run away to the smell and the sound of Tunapuna that the crowin' of a chicken in the Eastern Market provoke. And he use to come to the square every evenin' because it feel like the onliest place in the whole city of Port of Spain where people wasn't chasin' him down.*

*He was still sittin' on the runner with he long-bone hands hang down between he knees, admitting to heself that the cricket set the boys have was good. Three wickets make-up from saw-off broomstick, two bat, one make from coconut branch, the other a real store bat that still smell of linseed oil, and a cork ball what still had red paint on the surface. He get up and take up the ball and begin hefting it, throwin' it up in the air and catchin' it to feel the weight, while the other boys was watchin' him in silence.*

*In Tunapuna, he use to play with old tennis balls that rich people sell for six cents apiece after they lose they bounce. It was only at Saturday matches that he ever see a real cork ball like this one, and the* feel and the touch and the rough texture between he fingers, the bright red colour of the ball, give him a feeling of real power. He know rightway that he could bowl all of them down for 'duck' with this ball.

The boys and them look at him with a kind of questioning and then they begin movin' to they playin' and fieldin' position as they watch the thin boy count off fifteen paces. He turn round, and he foot slap at the turf, movin' him like a feather. He long thin body arch like a bow, the ball swing high in the air, he wrist turn in, and he deliver the shootin' red ball that turn pink as it race to the batsman. The batsman make a blind swipe and he miss; he head swing back quick to see how the ball gone pass so quick.

"Aye-I-aye," the wicketkeeper bawl out as the ball smack into he hands and make them red hot. The fielders who was scattered far off move in close close to see if they could catch the secret in he bowlin, but everytime he send the ball shootin' through the air, they miss some small flick of he wrist that make him bowl down all of them before they could see the ball.

"You want to come back and play tomorrow?" they ask him while they was standin' round the corner of Frederick and Prince Street, eating black pudding and souse from a vendor who had a charcoal brazier goin' on the street corner.

The boy jerk he shoulders up and down in a kind of indefinite gesture while he watch the other boys buy a inch, two inch, three inch of black blood sausage sizzlin' in a big tray on the pale red embers.

"How much you want?" the vendor ask him while he was starin' at the hot pink ashes in the mouth of the brazier, he thumbs hook in he pants waist. And he jerk he shoulders up and down again in the same indefinite gesture, and when it look as if the vendor was goin' to give him a piece of black puddin' for nothin, he move to the back of the clique of boys, and he disappear before the fat old woman turn round to look for him again.

It was turnin' that kinda salmon and orange light of the evening when the rays of the sun and the shadows of the trees in Woodford Square was playin' tug o' war, pullin' against each other til that final moment when nobody was lookin, and night fall on the groun' like a ball o' silk cotton sailing through the air til it touch the grass and settle there like if it was goin' to remain forever. The boy turn into they long tunnel gateway on Frederick Street and walk to the far end of the deep backyard.

*As he enter the room he smell cookin, the smoke from the kerosene lamps, fresh cut grass from he father clothes, and the faint smell of cig'rette and rum that he father body give off.*

*"Boy... where you does go whole evenin'? Why you don' stop home here and help your moomah?" he poopah ask he. The boy only see him late in the evenin' now, and every evenin' he bring home a nip of Black Cat rum. At first, the boy think that they was rich because that is what they say when they did leave Tunapuna where a nip of Black Cat rum did mean that it was a holiday or a fete where everybody was laughin' and makin' merry.*

*"Nowhere," he say as he hide the phial of firefly under the straw mat where he use to sleep.*

*"No way, no way... You beginnin' to play big shot! You could talk better than you moomah and poopah. Boy! You don't know how lucky you is to be goin' to school. When I was your age..." He poopah leave the sentence incomplete as he put the nip to he mouth and gargle the rum like if he was rinsin' out he mouth, then he swallow it.*

*"Leave the chile alone! If that is the way they teach him how to talk in school, that is the right way," he moomah say.*

*"Yes... but no way is a place? It have a place that call no way? Show me way no way is, show me! Way this boy does go and idle way he time. You know way he does go?" he poopah shoutin, and then it feel like one of them moment when he hold he moomah in front of he like a shield to save heself from a rain of blows.*

*He poopah fall back in one of them kinda silences. He did look like a old man nowadays. He let he hair grow on he head and he face unless they was goin' to Tunapuna. Then and only then he would get a shave and a trim, an' tell everybody how he was makin' big big money... how he was makin' three whole dollars a day at the Yankee base. He moomah was movin' about quick quick quick since she was finishin' up she cookin' for the evenin'. She look as if she get a sudden burst of energy that would make the whole evenin' preparation of they dinner come to an end with a soft breath and a sigh.*

*"The man for the room rent come, and he say that next month the price goin' up by two shilling," she say, like if she was talkin' to sheself. It was a damn small room they livin' in.*

*"It look as if everyt'ing goin' up since we come to live in town. Is always the same damn t'ing... Soon as you have a shilling save up... two*

*shilling expense come up. Soon as we did have a li'l money save up we have to go an' get a..."*

*"A chile?" he moomah ask.*

*The boy eyelid jerk up, and he eyes meet he moomah eyes, and he see she look back, pretendin' that she was lookin' at the fire in the brazier.*

*The same feelin' flood across he heart when he sit on the runner in the square, waitin'. Waitin' an' waitin' for somet'ing that he heself couldn't describe. When he leave the square that evenin, he did feel a kind of release from it; now it swallow he up again, clingin' to he eyebrow an' eyelash like them invisible cobweb that hangin' from the trees in the square in the early darkness of the evenin'.*

*"Boy, why you don't go and sleep instead of listenin' to big-people talk?" he poopah say, and the boy begin to get up from the low stool where he was sittin'.*

*"He ain't eat yet," he moomah say. "At least let him eat. What you want the child to do? Go out in the road so that he can't hear what you sayin? It only have one room, and the child have ears just like anybody else. Now you come and eat too before you drink anymo'."*

*The boy feel more and more that there was things about he poopah that he didn't notice before. Like the way he allow a long long silence linger between the moment when he talk, and then answer. An' durin' this lapse, he press he jaw teeth hard together to make a terrible grimace, then swallow hard before he talk again.*

*"Befo' I drink anymo'! Huh! It ain't have no mo' to drink," he poopah say as he turn the small green bottle upside down, and only two or three drops of the liquor fall on he tongue when he stick it out.*

*They did finish eatin' they dinner when he poopah say, "Boy, go an' full this cup with water at the standpipe." The boy unwind he long thin legs from the squattin' position he was in, and he hurry out to the standpipe in the yard, and he come back and hand the cup to he poopah.*

*"Alright, boy... go ahead now, go ahead an' sleep."*

*As he start to go over to the mat in the corner of the room, he moomah say, "Boy this... boy that. What happenin' to you at all? The child have a name, and it look as if you even forget that too."*

*He poopah let he body roll back slow slow slow, and when he was flat on the floor, he stretch out he limbs with a sigh of relief and tiredness. He eyeballs was dancin' in a frenzy under he close eyelids, then he talk up after a short silence.*

*"I too tired to argue with you, you hear, woman. I goin' to sleep so I could go and do the white-people work tomorrow, please God."*

*She turn down the lamp low and went out in the yard to wash the iron pot and enamel plate, and when she come back the boy could hear she talkin' to sheself like a habit she pick up nowadays, although she talkin' to he poopah, like if she was tryin' to cover over what she was sayin' in a kinda slant by not talkin' to him direct.*

*"Is true," she was mumblin', "that we aint save much... that you believe you workin' hard for nuttin'... but don't forget how much we had was to borrow to move to Port of Spain. One day, when we pay back everybody... we go be able to save somet'ing."*

*He thought he poopah was sleepin', but he hear he voice in the darkness.*

*"An' how much we have save up in the can?" She step outside the door and pull out two loose brick from the wall, and pull out the Capstan cigarette tin from where they use to hide they money, and she count out all the coin that they did save up after all the expenses since they come to the city.*

*"It have eight shilling save-up in the can," she say in a voice that the boy feel have a lot of disappointment in it. He poopah only let out a small noise like if he was dreamin' the incident, and then he fall off to sleep right on the floor.*

*The next evening the boy went to Woodford Square again. He was a lil bit late cause he had to go down to the foot of Frederick Street to buy somet'ing, and when he enter the square, he see the boys sittin' on the grass. The wicket was nail down in the groun' in readiness, the bats was leanin' up against a berry tree, and the ball was on the grass.*

*One of the boys spot he, and he shout out to the others, "Look, Bolan!" an' all of the boys stand up now. He begin runnin', full with a kinda excitement that he never feel before.*

*"We was waitin' fo you, man, what make you come so late today?" It make the boy feel so happy that they didn't start the game without him. He squeeze out a shiny red cork ball, brand new, from he pocket with a wide smile on he face, a smile that none of them ever see before. All of them run to they places, and they play cricket til it was dark in the square. The boy was goin' to be they star bowler from now on. And when they went to the vendor stand afterwards, he pay for all of the black puddin' they could eat.*

*"Gimmie a two inch piece," one of them call out, and the boy dig in he pocket, fingerin' the surface of the red ball everytime he reach for a coin to pay the vendor. Along the emptiness of Frederick Street they hear somebody callin'. All the boys look in turn to see if it was they parents callin' them, then they fall back to they black puddin'.*

*Suddenly, the boy recognise that it was he father in the cutaway trousers that come three-quarter way down he legs. "I have to go," he say hastily, and he run up Frederick Street. As he turn into the gateway where he livin', he father catch him by he ear, and he tug him close. "I goin' to give you a cut-ass that you go remember so long as you live," he say, as he lead the boy to the back yard where a old carpenter leave hundreds of switches of saw-off wood. The boy dance up and down when the lashes fall now on he foot, on he back next, and mo' lashes on he hands and he arms. And he father was shoutin' at he with every lash. "It aint have no t'ief in my family... We never rob nobody a black cent." The boy moomah was circlin' roun' them tryin' to catch the switch from he hand, and everytime she catch it, he take a new one from the big pile that on the groun'.*

*"All right!" he moomah say. "Nobody aint say that your family rob anybody... Why you don't leave the boy alone?" Everytime he moomah interfere and come to he defence, the boy get more stingin' lashes on he legs.*

*"And where this boy learn to t'ief from... Where? Where he learnin' all of these bad bad habit from... not me!" he poopah say.*

*"Don't call the chile a t'ief.... he not a t'ief... He just take the money to buy something."*

*"He is a damn t'ief... t'ief," he poopah insist, and the switch whistle with every word he sayin. "When I get trough with him, he never t'ief in he whole life again, he go remember... he go remember what it mean to be a t'ief."*

*The boy legs was mark up with thin red welts from the lashes, and now he stop jumpin' up and down from the switches. He poopah tired too, sweat runnin' down he neck, and he face, and now he moomah finally catch holda the switch in he hand.*

*"You aint have no feelin's in you... you done gone and kill the half of this boy that is your half... Now leave the half that make out of my body, if you still have any feelin's fo that."*

*She take the boy to the standpipe and mix some salt in a cup of water, and she make him drink it down, and then she take out the ball from he pocket, and the few pennies of change that remain.*

*She had gone to the square several days lookin' for the boy, and she did see he sittin' on the runner watchin' the other boys play, and she go away. When she see the red ball, she know the boys finally ask he to play with them.*

*"You still remember how to bowl?" she ask he. And the boy just nod he head, he eyes fasten to the groun'.*

*After they blow out the kerosene lamp, the boy roll and roll from one side of the mat to the other, tryin' to find a position where he body wasn't painful. He hear he moomah talkin' to he poopah in whispers, and he fraid that another argument, another beating go follow. He cover over he ears with he arms so he wouldn't hear they conversation, and long afterwards, when he fall asleep with he arms round he head, he dream that the big green man standin' in the cauldron of water in Woodford Square move he lips and talk to him. He say, "I didn't know boy, I didn't know... Is for you that we doin' all this... only you. We love you like nuttin' else in the whole whole world... mus always remember that."*

*And then when all of them wake up in the mornin, he wonder if he did dream the words that was still singin' in he ears... and then he remember the smell from he father body as he did come and lie down close to he durin' the night.*

Manko did not want to meet the woman next door, not this morning; he would see her in court. He would get dressed in his robes, get out in the yard and go down to Queen Street where some of the Chinese coffee shops were open, then he would go to answer his summons

The streets were quiet until he got to the market district where the coffee shops were, then the city seemed to come suddenly to life. All the vendors from the country districts were already there hawking their goods to the market vendors, and some of the country people seeing the preacher dressed in his robes greeted him with a respectful, 'Good morning, preacher.' He answered them without thinking, his thoughts filled with what would happen at the court house later on. Then when he had had his breakfast he walked slowly to the Magistrates' Court.

There were small knots of people standing about the courts, and they all made way for Manko to get past; some of them doffed their hats, and Manko raised his right hand in blessing to them, then he showed his summons to a policeman who pointed out the room where his case would be called, and as he entered the room he saw the woman and the policeman who served him the summons. They whispered back and forth in each other's ears and the woman began to cackle in the cupped palm of her hand. Manko turned his gaze away from them, and just then the bailiff made everyone stand as the magistrate entered and took his seat.

The court was filled with spectators. Some were people with nothing better to do who came to enjoy a few jokes as some villain was sentenced to jail. Others had come along with their friends to hear some case tried, and they would remain on to hear others. It was like going to the motion pictures, more amusing at times, as many of the cases were forced from the pathetic to the ridiculous, and sometimes the prosecutor as well as the magistrate went out of the way to ridicule the accused.

The magistrate was a very young man, thought Manko, but he was very stern. He had the first case called up. A man was accused of chicken-stealing, and out came a tired, sheepish-looking one-legged man on a crutch. He already wore the look of the condemned. The crowd at the back broke out in peals of laughter, so did the prosecutor, but the magistrate suddenly came down with his gavel and ordered quiet. There was murmuring and hissing, some people felt that the magistrate was not behaving properly. As the case went on, the complainant said that although the defendant was one-legged, he was the fastest runner in the city, and that further, he had a special knack of chasing down a chicken and then hurling his crutch at it with such accuracy that the bird did not have a sporting chance. The crowd broke out into loud guffaws again, and again the magistrate called for order. Finally, when the complainant asked the magistrate to make the one-legged man do a dance to prove how well he could ambulate with one leg, the magistrate leaned over and shouted to one and all, "If you think you have come here to make fun of justice and the law, you are mistaken... Not in my court." Then he turned to the bailiff. "Go back there in the dock and bring up anyone who thinks that all of this is funny." As the bailiff went back he assured the crowd, "There will be a ten shilling fine for anyone who thinks that these proceedings are for his humour. I am going to allow five minutes recess to clear the court of anyone who does not have any business here." Then he turned to the one-legged man and pronounced, "Case dismissed" as he went out of the room for recess.

But no one left the docks at the rear. There was grumbling; some people sucked their teeth in disgust, while others commented on how different it would have been with some of the older magistrates who had style. These young boys nowadays were too damn serious, and too damn officious in their positions. But when the magistrate returned, even more stern than before, they all quieted down. The next case was Manko's and during the recess the bailiff had placed him to sit with the woman and the policeman on the bench, and the crowd had already begun speculating and buzzing.

As the magistrate entered, the clerk called out, "All rise... All rise." Manko was so enveloped in his thoughts that he did not hear the clerk. The policeman who sat on the bench between him and the woman grasped the scruff of his robes and forced him to his feet. Meantime, amid the shuffle of people rising there was laughter from those who saw the policeman hang onto Manko's robes. The magistrate looked in the direction where the eyes were turned and saw Manko's face almost hidden in the collar of his robes, the policeman still holding onto the fabric above his head.

"What is your name?" the magistrate shouted to the policeman. The court was still standing. He had not bothered to tell them to be seated.

"Constable James," the policeman answered with a grin on his face, trying to draw the magistrate into the humour of the situation.

"And your number?" The policeman flinched. It was one of those things he could never remember. He had to look at the metal plaque on his shoulder to read off the number and he was having some difficulty doing so holding onto Manko's scruff as he was.

"Get your hands off that man, constable!" The policeman had not heard. He was reading off the numbers one by one and the magistrate stood up now and bellowed at him, "Constable James, are you deaf? I said to get your hands off that man!" The policeman let go of Manko's robes and the preacher's face stood out now, pale and drawn. He knew that he would not be able to speak if he was called upon. Let it be, he thought, let them think what they want to. Manko looked like a saint; resignation and humiliation showed through his eyes and there was a dead silence. Everyone waited to hear what had brought a preacher and a woman into court. The magistrate now asked everyone to be seated and he called up the policeman.

"Constable James, come up here and read your charges to the court." As the policeman entered the dock, the magistrate added, "and keep your hands off the defendant in my court... You fellows think that you make the law."

The policeman read off the charges made by the woman, in all the foul language which she used to report Manko, and then he added a few more obscenities which he claimed Manko shouted at him when he tried to deliver the summons. Manko closed his eyes at the words as they were read off; then he opened them. He looked at the woman and shook his head in despair.

She wore a bright little smile now, her lips all painted and her white teeth gleaming, and in her nervousness she began adjusting her blouse neck, then her buttocks on the seat, then her hair behind her ear-lobes, and when she looked at Manko again and still found his long sad gaze upon her, she began clearing her throat, then she could no longer bear it and broke out into a sharp twitter. The magistrate looked up at her and she pressed her hand to her mouth to suppress her giggle. The policemen, too, looked in her direction with some embarrassment. He already felt cut off from his role of the law; the magistrate had stripped him clean of that and ordered him about like a servant boy. He now sensed that this magistrate was not like the others who took the policeman's side automatically and joined in the heckling of the defendant.

"Will the two of you come up here?" The magistrate told the clerk to have Manko and the woman take the oath. Then they came and stood, one on either side of the policeman. "Now will you tell me what this is all about?" he asked the woman as he read through the summons again, and she began with a long tirade against Manko.

"My Honour..." she started out.

The magistrate winced as he looked at her. "Please... Your Honour," he corrected her.

"Please... My Honour," she began again, and the magistrate drew a deep pained breath of resignation. She stopped and watched him as he turned his eyes to the ceiling and clamped them shut, then he asked her to go on.

"My Honour, I can't have no peace in my own house night and day. This man who call heself a preacher won't let me have no peace. If he aint readin', he talkin', if he aint talkin' he watchin'..."

"Talking? Talking to whom?" the magistrate inquired.

"The parrot... Who else?" she said, as though it was the commonest thing in the world, then she turned to the parrot on Manko's shoulder and gave it a nasty glance. The magistrate shook his head and asked her to go on. "He always talking to that parrot, night or day, it don't make no difference, and what more, he teach the parrot to say all kinds of things from the Bible bout hell and sin and how God go punish me, and he only doing all of them things to pester my soul. From the time he move in the yard he only minding my business. If I go to the standpipe in the middle of the night to get a little water to drink he sitting down there watching me. If I go out to go bout my business, no matter what hour I come back, he still waiting up for me... I don't know what he want from me. If this keep up too much longer they go have to put me in the madhouse, My Honour."

The magistrate flinched each time she called him 'My Honour' but she went on in her complaint, which gained momentum as she spoke. The veins in her neck stood out and her voice took on the tone of the persecuted; it was left only for her to tell the magistrate that she had cramps in her body and aches in her bones because of the evil prayers that Manko was saying to punish her. Her own words had so moved her that she was feverish with emotion, the kind of exhausting emotion that made her mouth go dry and her breath come short and she had to break off to regain her self-control.

"Have you finished? Is that all?" the magistrate asked as she took a deep breath, her bosom and breasts heaving up and down. Humanity had always baffled the magistrate; perhaps he was still too young yet to know what the human heart was really like. Before him stood this tiny frail sinuous little woman; the constable was a huge hulking mass of a man, and yet this woman had no doubt been visited by hundreds, thousands, of men of this kind, for within her frail little body there was something which attracted men like this. And the preacher, what about him? Was he a peeping Tom? Had he simply made her afraid and ashamed of herself by moving in next door to her? It was no good, no good speculating like this, people invariably turned up such faces of innocence in the court, then when they got to the rum shops after their cases were tried, they laughed at the ways in which they were able to fool the judges. The woman was of this kind, and so was the constable. The magistrate was convinced of that, but the preacher baffled him. Was the man moved by something to go about spending his life like this? Or was he a faker? Manko's face was hard to read, he was not there to accuse, and he hardly cared to defend himself, he came to be judged. The magistrate hated this passivity; it threw all the weight of the responsibility upon him. He had to weigh, listen and try to determine just what was justice; true, his job was a simple one for the most part, everything was clear cut, he was just a magistrate. He might have sent someone up to the Royal Jail for six months hard labour who might have been innocent, but he had never had to try someone for his life. He longed for some case where all his faculties would be called upon, like this one, and yet he found himself wishing to be free of it. He heard the woman's voice very faintly saying, "My Honour... My Honour?" and he drew himself back sharply from his thoughts. "Yes," he said, looking at her again, and when she had his full attention again, "My Honour," she began again, "if that was all, I wouldn't be here today." She looked to the left and the right of the court and into the faces of the clerks. Then she turned to look at the faces at the back of the court as though she was embarrassed to speak the final words.

"A few days ago I catch him red-handed peeping at me through the holes in the wall between his room and mine, and it get so I fraid to take off my clothes in my own house." There, she had said it. Whether it was truth or lie she could no longer tell, it had become a heavy weight in her stomach until she got it out. And, as if to soothe some roughened spot in her mind, she felt the need to add, to push her statement even further along. "Ask anybody in the yard, My Honour," she demanded as proof of her accusations. "I had to get hammer-and-nail and cover up all the tiniest little holes in the wall to prevent him from peeping at my business." The crowd jeered, they whistled, some sighed, others groaned, and the magistrate came down with his gavel. "If this happens once more... once more, mind you, I am going to have the court cleared." The crowd took some time to quiet down, some of the men with devilish grins. There was something about a preacher peeping at a woman that tickled their imagination; others were with the preacher. "Naughty... naughty," they said to themselves, condoning the little mischief that these holy men will get themselves into with their fake abstinence. The hysteria was contagious, and the woman found it difficult to keep from bursting into laughter. The policeman, who knew her only too well, threw her reprimanding glances. He knew that if she burst out laughing now, all would be lost. He stood stiff at attention, his hat cradled in the crook of his arm, striving for composure and decorum. Was all of this really happening to him, he wondered. How did it get so out of hand? It seemed like a pleasant little favour he was doing her, the way a man gives trinkets to his mistress. He would get the preacher in court and then he would have to move out of the yard in shame, and they would have a good laugh over it for many nights as they romped with each other. But the woman was talking too much. She was giggling too much. And why did she have to volunteer all that talk? He did not like the way she went on and on, telling her troubles with that tinge of mischievous pleasure. And he was sure the magistrate only half-listened and half-believed her any way. If only they could have a little recess now, he could give her a few slaps in the corridor while no one was looking; that would knock some sense into her silly head.

When the crowd resumed its composure, the magistrate turned to Manko. "And what is your name?" he asked sternly. It was already implicit in his question that it was in bad taste for a preacher to appear in court for any reason, let alone this. "Are you a preacher?"

"I have been called into the service of the Lord God!"

No sooner had Manko replied than one of the clerks shouted at him, "Answer the question, man, yes or no!"

The magistrate brought down his gavel and silenced the clerk "Are you the magistrate in this court?" The clerk was silent, his head bowed, pretending to take notes on his pad. "Answer the question, yes or no when I speak to you! Are you the magistrate in this court?"

The clerk answered with a muted, "No, Your Honour." Then the magistrate repeated his question to Manko. "Are you a preacher?"

"Yes sir."

"And do you know this woman?"

"Yes sir, she is my next door neighbour."

"You have heard the charges... You're supposed to be a man of God and you come here accused of peeping at a woman through holes in the wall, using obscene language to an officer of the law, and attempting to prevent him from acting in his line of duty." He wished to punctuate his sentence with, "You ought to be ashamed of yourself." Guilty or not, a preacher should not be in court, it was in bad taste. No matter who a man was or what he did, he should never come to court, whether he was complainant or accused. One should conduct one's life in such a way that one was removed from any possibility of this kind. The mere fact that someone should accuse you of theft or assault, anything, was a black mark against you; it went down on the records and that was the end of that. You had a mark against you, you had been to court.

"Accused," said Manko, "but innocent, your Honour, let God be my witness." God indeed, thought the magistrate, who else could say that he did or did not witness what had happened. God indeed! That was a fine way to conduct one's defence. The magistrate was nettled by Manko's attitude. If he did not like people who babbled on and on, he disliked even more those who came into the court, his court, and stood there, just stood there and asked God to be their witness. What did they think the law was for? What did they think he was there for? What did they think the whole body of jurisprudence was about? One of the oldest, most ancient traditions which men, in their foolish ways, had had to construct to live decently amongst themselves because God never intervened. God indeed! God indeed! He wanted to come right out and ask Manko who was this God who had called him into His service. He wanted to ask him where that God was now? He did not understand how anyone could follow so blindly some simple conviction that would cause them to spend the rest of their lives going about asking people to be good, to lead clean lives. Each day of his life was filled with rogues and ragamuffins who stole, cursed, fought, lied. All of the vile things he had to listen to from day to day, and not one, not a single one, would ever change his ways. They came back time and again, if not for the same crime, then it was something else. God indeed! God indeed!

The parrot began squawking on Manko's shoulder. Manko wondered if the bird did not have some kind of human sense. Whenever its master was unsure of himself, if doubt ever crossed his mind, the bird began to caw. And what had set the bird off now, Manko knew, was that he had lied, not brazenly, but one of those half lies. He still felt that he could have awakened one night in his sleep and peered through the holes in the wall and seen the naked body of the woman. Also, when he caught the woman peeping at him and he went to the partition, he did peep in after slamming his hand at the hole, and he did see her crouched naked on the floor before she blew out the lamp. Could he tell that to the court? No! He decided to withhold it. He tried to calm Lorrito, whose noise was holding up the proceedings while the court waited.

The magistrate meantime saw his fears about this case becoming more and more real. It was going to be one person's word against the other. How could there have been any witnesses? And here was the preacher throwing the whole thing in his lap, resting calmly on his faith, his innocence. He detested Manko for this. Didn't he know that innocence had to be fought for, protected? It was never going to get up and speak for itself.

But somewhere deep within himself he felt that Manko was innocent; that the policeman and the woman were in some kind of collusion. When his temper flew to his head, he thought he would just let Manko suffer, let innocence and 'God be my witness' stand in their own shadows, while the world ripped them to pieces. That would be a good lesson! Then he saw that it would be no lesson at all. It would mean something to one man, just one insignificant creature, the world would never hear of it, nothing would be changed, others would still come day after day, year after year, basking in their innocence as though it had the power to do everything for them while they stood by with their arms folded.

Well, maybe he is innocent, but a damned fool as well, thought the magistrate as he searched his mind for a motive. What reason could the woman have to choose Manko to summon him for a disgraceful act like this? And it was suddenly clear to him as he looked at the coquetry in the woman's smile again. A woman like this would not want a holy man living next door to her. The very thought of a preacher living next door would be upsetting, even if they never spoke to each other. He was pleased with his analysis. His heart lightened and his brain warmed and his intellect was penetrating and clear as it went probing. The woman was afraid and ashamed of Manko, he thought. The woman must have believed that Manko was a real priest. This is why she wanted to get rid of him. And further, he thought, it was her faith, her belief in Manko that finally convinced him that Manko was not a fake. How interesting, he thought, how very interesting! Justice and the law became fascinating to him all over again. He felt the power and the responsibility of his office.

He looked up and saw the constable throwing cutting glances at the woman, which she ignored. She was pleased with herself and the way the case was going. She was beginning to feel she could have handled this all by herself Her big, rough-talking policeman was not rough-talking at all. He had only to enter the court and face a magistrate and he was a little cowering boy again, the way they all were. Well, that was his business. She was not afraid of court houses or magistrates, she felt like an actress in a humorous play, making the audience laugh with her every word and gesture. She wore a tight little smile as she looked up saucily at the magistrate. She was convinced that he favoured her in his own stern, rebuking way. That's the way men were, all of them. They loved to play angry and shout a little and play boss until you let them feel that they were the boss, then they showed their real selves, the cuddling little boys they were! Didn't she see this all the time? Hadn't she held some of those huge strong he-men cradled in her arms, watching them nuzzle at her little breasts while she stroked their heads and calmed all the fury that they had in them? She looked straight up to him and cocked her head to one side with a little coquettish smile. The magistrate became infuriated with her. Make a joke of the law, would she! Spend five shillings for a morning's entertainment... Well, not in his court. And now she had the brazenness to be cocky with him too. He had tried to keep personal things out of the case. He tried to keep from questioning her character and respectability. Now he lashed out at her:

"Have you ever been intimate with this man?" he asked her outright.

"Who me, My Honour?" she cried in surprise and alarm, looking at Manko. "Oh Gawd, I never hear such a thing in my life. Me, My Honour?" she repeated, looking Manko up and down.

The magistrate became even more infuriated with her because she now had a sly little grin at his suggestion that she could have been intimate with a holy man. The very thought tickled her and she was about to add that the idea had never entered her mind when the magistrate stood up now in disgust.

"I do not mean with the preacher, madam, I mean with the constable!"

Her head fell, she hemmed, she hawed, and then she looked up and said, "I don't know what you mean, My Honour... I don't know what you mean by that word... How you call it?"

"Intimate!" the magistrate bawled, then spelt it out with even more anger and disgust in his voice. "I-n-t-i-m-a-t-e."

"I don't know what you mean and besides I don't know how to spell." The crowd had slowly built up to this as though they waited for the right moment. They all burst out into loud guffaws and peals of laughter which could be heard all the way down St. Vincent Street. There was no doubt in the magistrate's mind that several of the other court rooms would have had to hold up their proceedings because of the noise coming from **his** court. Some of his colleagues would, no doubt, meet him in the corridors later on and ask with an air of innocence what had happened and who was it that conducted his court like that. He came down sharply with his gavel and kept rapping until there was silence. "I want this court cleared of everyone," he ordered his bailiffs, and the other clerks and everyone ambled out, dragging their feet and sucking their teeth in disgust and disappointment as he sat down wearily. He said, more to himself than the woman, "You're an abomination."

She sucked her teeth at him again. "I dunno what that mean."

"You're ill-mannered and ill-bred," he added, and before she could say that she did not know what he meant by that, he turned on her. "When you thought I asked you if you were ever intimate with the preacher, you knew exactly what I meant, but suddenly you became ignorant when I ask you if you have ever been intimate with the constable."

She paused and put her hand on her hip, looking straight up at him. She was no longer her calm, cajoling self. Anger had overtaken her and she was thoughtless of any outcome now.

"When you ask me that... that word bout preacher, I had to answer no because even if I don't know the meanin' of the word, I never had nuttin' to do with him," she said, filled with injured pride.

"We will see about that," he said, as he had the bailiff make the constable take the oath, and as soon as the constable finished, the magistrate warned him, reminded him, that failure to tell the truth would result in grave consequences involving his job, his superiors who would get to hear and his family and friends who would be dragged in to vouch for his character. All of these images ran through the constable's mind as he stood in the box, looking first at Manko, then at the woman, and then he was put right to the point.

"Have you ever been intimate with this woman?"

"Yes, Your Honour," he replied simply, somewhat humbly and ashamed, no longer being able to look Manko or the woman in the eye.

"That is all," said the magistrate. "But before I dismiss this case I order you both to pay fines of five pounds each to the court for wasting its time, and you are further ordered to pay costs of twenty shillings each to this man for inconveniencing him. Case dismissed!"

Manko began to stammer something about not wanting to take any money from them, but the magistrate looked him firmly up and down and simply told him never to appear in court again, not in any court, as he put it, stalking out of the room in disgust.

His refusal to accept the payment for the damages left him with a strange sense of wellbeing, of power, if not his power, the power of God and the way His hand had worked. He had forgotten the little lie he told and each time it surfaced in his mind, he cast it out. He had said to the magistrate: "Let God be my witness" and that was enough. As he moved through the city a vast number of emotions gripped him. He was now indignant and filled with disgust. Hate filled his step and his walk as he headed for Calvary Hill where he hoped his mind would quiet and calm itself. He was innocent, so why did he have to be dragged and paraded in court? Why? Why was this kind of evil possible? Were people so possessed with the devil that he had to be routed out of them with force and violence? But then he thought of Miss B., who also lived in the yard, and what a good woman she was.

*She had ambition, she had she own kind of ambition, and when we go all aroun' the yard, we will see that everybody in the yard had ambition. When the preacher come into the yard, Miss B. was the first one who like him. She like him because anybody who come out from the orphanage come out straight like a pin, and Miss B. was one of them people who could see from the way a man walk an' from the way he talk that he straight like a pin. Now, Miss B. had she own ambition. She had four children and all of them sleepin' in the same little barrack room. Miss B. use to make them dress up good. She would starch and iron they clothes even if it take she til twelve o'clock in the night when the Trinity Church was striking out the bells. She want she children to be somebody. Everybody want to be somebody down in Trinidad. The preacher walk into the yard that day and he had long white robes, he had the big Bible in he hand and he had he parrot on he shoulder. Miss B. like him right away, she want to have people in the yard who goin' to further that ambition that she have. Now what Miss B. ambition was was not so much for sheself but for she children, but children never want to do what big people tell them to do. She had a son, and he name Tommy. When Tommy come home from school, she use to tell him: "Go inside the house and take off my clothes and put on your clothes."*

*She take the boy to school the first day. She was one of them parent who does take a great amount of responsibility when they take they child to school. So when she take the boy to school and she say she want to see the principal, the principal damn glad because nobody come in to talk wid him about they children. So Miss B. say to the principal one small thing. She say: "This boy mind belong to me, and he body belong to you. And if he can't learn, is he body that I handin' over to you so that you could make a gentleman out of him."*

*One day Tommy run out of the house, and it was the rainy season and he come back home and he clothes drippin' wet, and he mumma say to him, "Where you went; it look as if you was standin' up in the sunshine?" So Tommy standin' there in the rain, and he head hang down and Miss B. look at him and he can't even lift up he eyes to look at she. She let him stand up there in the rain for about three, four minutes, then she tell him, "Come inside the portico."*

*Now it have somet'ing in Trinidad that we call a grater. Is somet'ing that people does grate coc'nut on, and somet'ing that they does grate nutmeg on, and somet'ing they does grate corn on, and is a big size grater, not one of them little ones that you does see nowadays. It make from big piece of tin can, and it have a fellah who have a hammer an' a nail, and he make a few hundred holes in this sheet of tin can, and he put it on a nice frame of hardwood and he go aroun' Port of Spain and he sell them to everybody. So Miss B. say to Tommy, "Come here, boy, and kneel down on this grater." Tommy know what that mean, he had to kneel down on the grater before. He put he knees on the grater, and he still holdin' he head down, and Miss B. say, "How much time I tell you not to go out in the rain so you would catch the four-day fever and come in here and give me more work?" She want the boy to be a straight-pin. Tommy can't look up at she, he know damn well that if he look up he gonna get somet'ing else. He kneelin' down on the grater and he holdin' he head down. Well, the boy wasn't goin' to lift up he head and look at she, and she wasn't goin' to stand up there and wait for him to do it. She was cookin' dinner, and she just went on stirrin' this pot and that pot. When she finish, she put down the pot-spoon. She still facin' the two pots, the boy still kneelin' down on the grater. Miss B. still had she back turn to him, she still don' want to look at him. She say, "Where you went? Why you does go an' play in the rain.?" The boy feelin' every single hole in that grater cuttin' he knees. He didn't say a word. So Miss B. ax him again, "Where you does go an' waste your time? Where you went?" The pot was boiling over; Miss B. take up the pot spoon and she stir it aroun' a little bit, and the sauce boil down, and she put the lid a little bit halfway so it wouldn't boil over again, but she still wouldn't look at the boy and the boy still holdin' he head down, so she put the spoon next-side to the two pots and she still waitin'. She ax him again, "Where you does go? Where you does go playin' in the rain?" And somet'ing happen in the boy.*

*"I went to play wid me friends!" he shout out to she. Miss B. turn aroun' and she had a smile, a grin on she face like nobody in the yard ever see before. She give him a backhand slap right across he mouth, and he feel every knuckle bone in she hand. The inside of he mouth bust open, and he put he tongue on the spot, and he taste he own blood. It taste a little bit like iron, and a little bit like salt. He did want to spit it out, but he know better... He swallow it.*

*"What yuh say?" she ax him. "Who yuh say yuh does go play with?" And that somet'ing still boilin' up in the boy, it boilin' up just like the pots Miss B. have on the coals.*

*"I does go to play wid me friends, me friends," he shout back. Miss B. give him another backhand on the other side of he mouth.*

*"I is the only friend you have... I want you to remember that as long as yuh live. Yuh understand? I is the onliest, onliest friend yuh have in the whole wide world, and I don't want you to ever forget it." The boy head hang down, he put he tongue on the other cheek inside he mouth and he taste the same t'ing, salty and iron, and he swallow it again.*

*It had a bleach in the yard make out of a lotta big stone that people put there so that when they wash they clothes they could stretch them out on the stones in the hot sun, so that when they rinse them all of the dirt come out of the clothes.*

*Miss B. went to the bleach, and she get two big-stone, and she say to Tommy when she come back wid it, "This is for you." Tommy look up for the first time and he eyes meet hers. She tell him, "Stretch out your hands." And he stretch out he hands, parallel to the groun'. She put one stone in he left hand and one stone in he right hand.*

*The preacher was sitting in he doorway because the rain was still falling, and he was reading his Bible. Miss Violet was home because the light was on. Mr. Harry didn't come home from work yet. Everybody hear what Miss B. say to the boy and everybody see how she give him two big stone in he hand. And the preacher know that it is not he business. Miss Violet couldn't hear what was goin' on anyway. So the boy was kneelin' down on the grater with the two big stone in he hand. One of the other pots boil over. Miss B. stir the pot a little bit more and then, when she see that everyt'ing was finish, she take the two pots off the coal-pot and put them down and she make the boy get up and she tell him that it have a box of salt right inside the house and he should get the box of salt, and put some salt in some water. The boy didn't do anything. So she ax him, "You hear what I say? I say take some of the salt and put it in some water in a basin and kneel in that!" The boy aint say nothin, he still can't talk. She rush over and grab him by the ear, "Yuh hear what I say?" she was shoutin' right into his ear.*

*The boy say, "Yes, Ma," and he get the salt, and he get the basin and he put the salt in the water.*

*Miss B. say, "Mix it up, now, mix it up, mix it up good." The boy stir the salt in the water, and she say, "Now kneel down in that, and when you get t'rough, I want you to go over to the preacher." And the boy didn't say anyt'ing again. She say, "Yuh hear what I tell you? I want you to go over and talk to the preacher when you get up from here."*

*The boy say, "Yes, Ma... Yes, Ma." And when the boy kneel down in the saltwater and the saltwater get into all of the million little cuts that it have on he knees, he know that if he flinch one eyelash, Miss B. would put him on that grater again. So he kneel down in the saltwater and say, "Yes, Ma." And when Miss B. say, "I want you to go over and talk to the preacher," he say again, "Yes, Ma."*

*It have three special schools in Port of Spain: Piccadilly, Grosvenor and Nelson Street, and if you want your son to turn out to be somet'ing, to make somet'ing of he life, you send him to one of these schools because the teachers in them schools know how to make a boy straight like a pin. When they givin' you dictation, they walkin' up and down the aisle, and they lookin' over you shoulder to see if you spellin' the words right, and if they see that you spell a word wrong, bam! you get a lash on you shoulder, you don't know why, you don't know which word it is and it aint finish there, because when the dictation over, you have to switch papers wid somebody who sittin' nex' to you. Then the teacher spell out all of them words, and every wrong word that you have on that paper, you get three lashes in the palms of you hand. That is number one at them schools. Number two is the mornin' befo' the school-bell ring. The boys playin' cricket and they playin' football in the yard, and all of the teachers come outside wid they long strap. The strap about three feet long and about an inch wide, and they keep it soakin' in a little basin of water. Some of the boys say that the teachers use to have it soakin' in pee, because that way the strap does give you a better sting when it lash you. It had some teachers who use to have a cane that they could bend end to end and it wouldn't break. So the teachers an' dem would stand up outside in the yard and wait for the school-bell to ring, and as soon as it ring, it look like one big ant-hill, everybody runnin' from one place to another, an' licks flyin' left and right, and although it had a lotta boys who could run damn fast, them teachers was some damn good runners too. And they would be swingin' these canes, and they would be swingin' these straps and the boys had was to line up. First standard line up over here, second standard line up over there, third standard line up over there, and in about two minutes flat, every single class line up, straight-like-a-pin. Then the teachers, each one of them that have one of the classes, walkin' up and down the line and if a boy standin' up with he head hangin' down, or if he standin' up a little bit crooked, too much on the left foot or too much on the right, bam! another lash and he straighten up and he hold up he head, and that is the way they make a gentleman out of you if you go to Grosvenor or Piccadilly or Nelson Street Boys. Well, we don't want to say exactly which school this boy went to because we don't want the school to get a bad name.*

*Now we say that everybody have ambition in Trinidad. And we say that Miss B. have she own kind of ambition. She ambition was for these children, she ambition was that when she get old they will take care of she, so she want them to make somet'ing of theyself. And let the reader know that this boy, when he grow up, get to be manager of a Ford Motor Agency. He was one of the best mechanics in town, he get promoted and he get to be manager of the whole agency and he use to drive aroun' in a big Ford and he take care of he mumma just like she did want it to happen. Some people wouldn't understand how to make a boy straight, and some people would t'ink that a boy like this boun' to go bad, but it just go to show you how well people understan' they own. Miss B. had all of the right ideas, and she make this boy into a gentleman, and you could go down to Port of Spain any day and go to the local Ford agency and ask for Tommy. And if you see him, and you ask him, "Boy, what happen to you? You remember them days when you Mumma use to beat you?" Tommy would laugh, and he would tell you how well he takin' care of he mother nowadays, and if you see he mother, you never believe that she was the kinda woman who work so hard to bring up these children in the world.*

*The idea that God dead was not one Miss B. believe in; he very much alive. Miss B. want to make sure that this boy know that God is a very real man and he livin' out there, and she want him to go to the preacher if only to let him remember, to let him know that every time he think that he goin' to do somet'ing wrong, it have somebody upstairs there lookin' out for him, watchin' on him, spyin' on him and that no matter what he do, he go have to answer for it, whether it in hell or heaven or right here on earth. And since Miss B. didn't know which of these two places she would end up in, she want to make sure that this boy get to be straight like a pin here on earth. So she want him to go over to the preacher to hear a few of the good words of the Lord so that he will straighten up and he will remember them for the rest of he life.*

*Rain it come peltin' down, it ring out on the galvanize roofs. The long thin threads bring out a primitive instinct in man, woman and child. The pushcart driver was sittin' in he doorway. The yard is a place that hold no secret. The preacher did see the boy, his arms stretch-out with the big stones, kneelin' down on the grater, and he hear Miss B. tell he to go and talk with the preacher so he could learn the ways of God.*

*Miss Violet was also sittin' in she doorway lookin' out at the rain. She did always like all of the children in the yard. Every child remember how she would give a kiss to the candy vendor, and he would give he goods to the children at half-price. Times like that make she remember when she was a child, make she remember when she had only twelve years, exactly the same age like Tommy. Miss Violet look at the pale grey ragged threads of rain, and somet'ing inside of she say somet'ing, the same somet'ing that the rain say to the preacher and the pushcart man, although none of them* ***know*** *exactly what the rain say, know in* *the sense that they would take some kind of action, like interfere with Miss B. and Tommy and he punishment. But what Miss Violet understand was that she was going to compensate this boy for he sufferin' and pain, she would make him learn what love does feel like.*

*T'ree days later, when the wounds, the cuts in the boy's knees heal up; t'ree days later and Miss B. had to go to a midnight mass; t'ree days later and the pushcart driver went to bed, closed his doors at an early hour; t'ree days later and the preacher (who wondered bout past and present, dream and reality, who did not know whether he did peep through the hole in the wall and see Miss Violet' body, or whether he dream that reality), the preacher had left that evenin' to search for solace in the Britannia Bar. Whether Miss Violet plan on havin' any visitor that evenin' we cannot know. Whether Miss Violet plan to teach love to this boy because of that moment, we will not insist pon that. Whether it is possible to have one's life completely transformed by a moment, as was the case with Miss Violet when she first find love, and whether it was that moment when Miss B. was punishin' this boy that Miss Violet decide she would not have customers that evenin, we will not say that either. We will simply say that these t'ings, like so many t'ings, are moments where several t'ings happen at the same time. The boy come back from Woodford Square; he playin' football with he friends, he sweatin' and he tired with the kinda exhaustion a young body understand.*

*As he enter the yard, Miss Violet see him. As he about to pass she door, she say, "Tommy, you remember de time when the candy-man come and you didn't have no money and you did want to get a piece of candy?"*

*The boy say, "Yes," and he laughing, and Miss Violet laugh too.*

*Then she say, "You had anyt'ing to eat yet?" and Tommy just shake he head and hol' down he head like he always use to do. And Miss Violet say, "You want to come in here and eat somet'ing wid me?" and the boy just nod he head and he walk inside Miss Violet room.*

*It had a table and two chairs. It had a bureau with a picture on top a' it of a man and a woman. Tommy believe that they must be Miss Violet' mumma and puppa. It had a radio with a record-player and some calypso records next to it, and it had a bed.*

*Tommy was lookin' at the bed because he never sleep in a bed in he whole life. She did make some black-eye peas and rice earlier on during the day, and when she was in the shop, she did get a little hambone and she take de hambone and cut off all the little pieces and she put in the whole bone after she crack it up wid a big stone from the bleach. So she give the boy somet'ing to eat and de boy lookin' at she for the first time.*

*She say to him, "Tommy, you ever see what a girl look like underneath she clothes?" Tommy hang down he head again. Miss Violet went to the doors and she close them and she start takin' off she clothes. And when Tommy lookin' off to the side, Miss Violet come over to him and put she fingers on he chin and she hold he head up so that he eyes lookin' right into she eyes. And then she take off another piece of clothing, and she watchin' de boy, and this time when she get completely naked, the boy lookin' now, he aint lookin' away like he was lookin' away before. She walk over to him and she take he right hand and she put it on one of she breast. The boy hold he hand on she breast and she have she own hand on top of he hand because the boy don't know what to do. Miss Violet squeeze the boy hand so that the boy hand squeeze she breast. What happen was the same t'ing in reverse. Miss Violet breast send a electric shock in the boy hand and the electric shock went from the boy hand to Miss Violet hand, and from she hand to she own body. After she do that, she take the boy hand away and she hold him by he head and she bring he head to she chest, and the boy cheek resting on she breast. She was standin' up and the boy sittin' down on the chair after he finish eatin' the black-eye peas and rice. She turn he head aroun' and she put he mouth right on top of she breast and then she take the nipple of she breast and she put it in the boy mouth. The boy taste she nipple and Miss Violet didn't have to tell him what the to do. The boy begin to suck the nipple, like if he was a baby drinkin' milk. And then Miss Violet hold him very gently by the head and move he mouth over to she other nipple and the boy suck she other nipple again like if he never had milk in he whole life. She ax him, "You had enough to eat, Tommy?"*

*And he say, "Yes, Miss Violet."*

*She say, "You want to go home now?" And the boy hang down he head, he couldn't answer.*

*He didn't have no buttons on he shirt but he had two straight-pin to keep the shirt' close. He didn't have no buttons on he pants but he have a safety-pin to hold them up. Miss Violet take out the straight-pins from he shirt, one by one, and she take off he shirt and she hang it up on the other chair. Miss Violet take he hand and put it between she legs, and while she holdin' he hand between she legs, with the other hand she openin' up the safety-pin of the boy's trousers until she take the trousers off, and then she take him by the hand and walk him over to the bed. She laid him down on the bed. The boy look at she, the boy look at she back as she walk over to the lamp and she turn it real low, but he could still see the shape an the form of Miss Violet body. She come over to the bed and she kiss him between he legs and then she lay on top of him and she take him inside of she. She take him inside of she in such a way that she wasn't restin' the weight of she whole body on top of him, and before long the boy begin to move inside of she and Miss Violet stop and she turn over and she make the boy get on top of she. She open she legs and she make the boy take he t'ing in he hand and put it inside of she, and the boy love she that night.*

*When they finish, she put he clothes back on and she put the safety-pin back on and she put the straight-pins back on and she look at the boy and the boy look at she and she kiss him on he forehead. She open the door and the boy went outside and then she close the door and she stretch out in the bed and she had a good cry that night.*

Manko stopped in at a rumshop to look at the faces of people and all he saw there were wretched people living out their wretched lives. They couldn't be cajoled. They needed to be dragged through the streets by their scruffs before they understood God.

There were the usual cliques of men and an occasional woman drinking in the rumshop, and in the corner of the shop sat five people, four men and a woman at the only set of chairs and table. They looked up as Manko entered. They pushed their hats and caps higher up on their foreheads, looked Manko up and down, then one of the men pulled his cap over his eyes and slouched deep down in his chair and sent a long stream of spit flying. The others laughed. The woman cackled and they went on with their drinking. Manko stood by himself drinking his rum, tempted to look in their direction, but he could only hear the filthy language they were tossing back and forth and each time he overheard one of their obscenities he winced and put down his glass. He couldn't even drink his rum in peace. The man at the table would look about and it seemed to Manko that their eyes met through some kind of compulsion, and each time their eyes met the man arched a stream of his spit through his front teeth straight into the spittoon, then started cursing. Manko became so infuriated that he spilled his drink as he rushed over to the man and collared him.

"You ugly beast... you aint have no respect!" he told the man, holding onto his collar firmly. "Every word you utter is just as rotten as your insides... You aint have no shame even in the presence of a messenger of God!" A few of the other drinkers came running over to restrain Manko. So did the proprietor of the rum shop.

The man, meantime, looked sheepish and ashamed.

"You know how it is, preacher," the proprietor tried to calm Manko, "They have troubles and they come in here to ease they mind. A few words can't hurt nobody."

Manko became even more indignant. He wanted to make the villain go down on his knees as he had done with the workman at Calvary. The man's friends now began to coax him. "Go ahead and tell the preacher you sorry, boy."

"He shouldn't only be sorry... he should repent for the black soul he have," Manko demanded.

"Let him go this one time, preacher; he didn't mean it, he forget where he was, that is all," one of the men in the group pleaded with Manko, and the man himself, wishing to end this scene as quickly as possible, knelt down on the floor and asked Manko's forgiveness.

"Excuse me, preacher, I didn't mean to use all that nasty language," he said to Manko who towered above him, looking at his slumped shoulders.

"Get up now, you damned rogue, and pray to God to wash that black tongue of yours." Then Manko went back to the counter where the proprietor rushed to wipe up the spilt drink and refill his glass.

"On the house," he told Manko, who stared straight ahead as though the injury and the insult was too much to be calmed with a mere free drink.

With this insult, this injury, this desire to seek revenge, God's revenge, Manko left the rum shop for Calvary Hill. He had known the sensation before; his senses were sharpened, his vision invaded by stark bright colours. His ears picked up the minutest sounds and his skin felt sensitive to the point of pain. He stalked through the streets as though indeed on an errand, an errand of God. He ground his teeth and his entrails answered back with the same grinding movement and his pace did not lag until he reached the foot of Calvary, where he saw the cross of gold, all freshly painted and shining in the evening sun. He stood before the cross and laid his great Bible open in front of him, and stood in silent meditation as he caught his breath from the climb.

Two elderly women on their way home from the market stopped to see what was happening, and when Manko opened his eyes and saw them, he shouted from the depths of his lungs, "I beseech you in the name of the Lord God to repent."

The old women crossed themselves and laid their baskets down. The zig-zag road up to Calvary was used by the people of the district as a short cut to their homes on the hills beyond, and, as the city emptied out, several people heard the preacher's voice and they stopped to listen. The spirit had so moved Manko that he let his voice fling out to them.

"And when the day of judgement come... which side of the Lord will you be sitting on... his left side... or his right side?"

The crowd had grown and there were some twenty people standing around Manko, some out of pure curiosity, while some of the older folk answered his threats and warnings with 'Amens'. There was a group of five or six young men in the back who whispered among themselves and Manko eyed them crossly. Then someone came up the hill whistling, and they all turned to hail out to one of their friends who joined them. Others shushed them so that the preacher could go on.

"And if any of you think that it is easy to get past the gates of heaven..." Manko began again, but again the clique at the back interrupted.

"Why the hell you don't go out and look for work... you damned idler!"

The remark stung Manko like a blow; he could not think of words fast enough and the comment had so amused others in the crowd that they began laughing. The tide turned and the spell was broken. People shook themselves as though they suddenly remembered the house cleaning they had to do, the fires that they had to start and the dinners they had to cook.

"It aint have no hope for you young rascals in the world today." Manko finally roused himself to reply. "You have no respect for anything... not even the Lord God who wants to give you a chance to repent before you get up there." And he jerked his index finger, pointing to the cross.

An elderly man leaning on a cane in the crowd was nettled by this remark. His son was among the clique of young men, and, true, maybe the boys cursed and they gambled and they chased after girls, but so what? He'd been young once too. Besides, his son was taking care of him now in his old age; what more could you ask? His son was a good boy as he saw it; who was this fool to come along and criticise? The old man felt sure that Manko was neglecting his duties to *his* tired old parents somewhere.

"Young fella like you!" he shouted. "You crazy or what? All you could do is go around digging up other people sins... Leave that for an old man like me. Young fella like you, you young and strong and you don't know how to enjoy life... walking about with a long long face and all you want to do is talk with God." The old man turned to face the crowd as he spoke his last sentence. "You ever hear more?"

The crowd split now, as though someone had gone through it with a knife and crisscrossed back and forth, leaving little cliques mumbling among themselves. Several people were already on their way as they met others coming up the hill, who enquired what all the commotion was about; they simply said that there was a mad man under the cross preaching a lot of nonsense. One woman coming up the hill was still curious to see with her own eyes what was going on. She forced her way in front of Manko. Her face was one of those that have a look of perpetual disgust as she looked Manko up and down about three times. This direct confrontation disconcerted Manko; the woman stood only inches away from him, going over her thoughts. She had one illegitimate daughter from a father who'd absconded, and now her daughter was about to repeat her example.

"But look at what happening in the world dese days, huh!

Plenty nice nice girls can't find a man to get married, and look at this worthless scamp playing preacher... You ought to be ashamed of yourself, boy, you ought to be ashamed," she repeated as she walked away. As she ambled off; so did the remaining handful of listeners, leaving Manko alone in front of the cross.

Miss Violet, meantime, was fed up with everything and she told the policeman just that. She told him that he was not a man, "No man at all," that he was a coward and for all of his big talk he was not worth a damn. She did not know who she hated most.

Manko had disappeared, the magistrate had stalked out, and when they went to pay the fines the constable had no money, so she had to dig into her purse to pay them both. When they got out in the street she told the policeman to go to hell, she did not want to see him again, she had a headache and she was just plain sick of men... "All of them... they just the same."

Yet when she left the policeman and went to the rum shop at the corner and she saw a woman drinking by herself, though she went up to join her, they just stood there in silence, each one drinking quietly. It was as though they could scent something similar about themselves, perhaps that they were both the kind of women who did not care too much for the company of their own sex. They said nothing to each other, although they were dying to tell their own troubles. They both left the rum shop together, smiling foolishly; they had not gotten into a quarrel or an argument, left as the best of friends, yet each simply nodded at the: other and went on their separate ways, they both knew, to another rum shop in search of that unsated, unknown thing buried in their hearts.

As she went past the rumshop that she always went to, she looked in and saw Manko. There was a man kneeling in front of him, and others restraining him. She couldn't even drink her rum in peace now. There was something about going to the same rum shop year after year, and the thought that someone, anyone, could prevent her from going there when she wanted to was enough to make her head fly off; she felt not only pursued and harried by this preacher, but swallowed up by him.

She roamed the streets until she came to one of those wretched little bars near the bus station which, though crowded at some hours, remained empty in their own darkness most of the time. She didn't like the place; it smelt of acrid disinfectant and all the sweat of harried people who had caught their buses and gone home and left their body odours behind in the bar. There was a little twisted crippled man who always stayed on at this rum shop; just as she had her rumshop, so this was his. He doffed his hat to her when she entered. She drank down lime juice with four aspirins and a tall glass of white puncheon rum, Immediately she felt its fires in her stomach she felt better.

"It look as if you have troubles, darlin'," the cripple said to her. She was disgusted with his looks; his face was all contorted when he tried to smile his saucy smile. She looked at him as though she were examining his entire being, and then a great feeling of tiredness overtook her and she felt like crying.

"Yes," she said. "If you only knew my troubles... I can't begin to tell you how rotten people is in the world today."

The cripple did not say a word, but he simply nodded his head in agreement. His expression took on all the sadness of humanity, and in his deep sunken eyes alone he was giving assent to her view of its rottenness. He knew it all, what was there to say? He could only agree with her, he could only nod and assume some of her burden.

"Why you don't come over here and talk to me a little... It so quiet in here," she said. And the cripple, who liked this bar, who liked it for the lonely stray who came in from time to time, moved over and listened to her until she had unloaded all her woes, drinking steadily and filling up his glass as they went on and on. "What a world... what a bad world... That is the way people is... What else you could expect in this world today... People too damn worthless minded... Where you ever find anybody who give a damn for you...? Laugh and the world laugh with you... cry and you cry alone." On and on they chatted until something deep within the two of them had cooled and subsided, and then the cripple edged his knee against hers and she looked at him with surprise, and her heart was filled with disgust, disgust for herself because she knew she had done something to him, that she had taken something from him and that she was not going to be able to pay the price.

Neither she nor Manko knew that the word had gone around in the yard, but everyone knew the details and the outcome of the case. For the most part the residents did not take sides, although some of the women thought that she was brazen. They liked the idea of having the preacher in the yard. He was a quiet man who, without a word, had brought a kind of respectability to it. If someone in the yard came home with a little too much rum under his belt, he straightened up and stopped staggering, and when he got home and his wife began abusing him for his drunken ways, he would say, "Shhh... remember we have a preacher livin' in the yard, don't start usin' bad words before he hear you."

But that was all right for some people. The woman had no one to answer to. She sang to herself as she cooked out in the yard, she poured from her bottle in broad daylight, and she always had a smile for everyone. As she walked home through the streets, she felt a surge of emotion flood through her for the way she had run away from the cripple, and as she walked through the dim streets she became all choked up, tears welled in her eyes and when she tried to laugh, she was both laughing and crying at the same time. Each time her throat tightened up she forced the laughter to come; there was no one in the streets and she indulged herself in this little game of tug of war that her body played on her, and to her surprise, as she got closer to home, she began feeling much better. But as she went through the events of the day, the thought of entering the yard made her sullen and she liked herself much better this way. She turned into the yard and the pushcart man who lived in the last room came running up to her. He had hidden six shillings in a crevice of the wall beside his room and now it was gone. She simply sucked her teeth. "You think that I have time to bother bout you six shillings? You don't think that people have nuff troubles of they own?"

The pushcart man knew that she was up at all hours and might have seen if anyone was poking around the wall at the back of the yard. Why did he have to bury his money in the wall? He had thought that if he left it in his room someone might steal it and now, even though he had gone to such pains to remove one of the stones in the wall, place his money in a cigarette tin and embedded it in there, it was gone. He became angry at her indifference, at her cutting tone. Six shillings meant nothing to her; she didn't have to work like he did to get six shillings saved up, and he told her so.

"What you mean I don't have to work like you to make six shillings?" she asked hotly.

"You know what I mean... You want me to spell it out? You always walking about in the yard in the middle of the night..." Suddenly it was clear to him that it was she who had stolen the money. "I know your footsteps well," he insisted, "and I hear you come and thief my money."

Some of the yard dwellers poked their heads out of their doors to hear what was going on, others stood in their doorways waiting to hear the outcome. Well, that was the way it was, a troublemaker was a troublemaker; it was bound to happen; first the preacher, now the pushcart man; who knew what she would be up to next.

"You better mind you' mouth before I get a policeman to arrest you for accusing decent people, you hear?" she warned him, her voice shaking with indignation. She was exhausted from the day's troubles, she had nothing left in her, and this man was scraping at the raw edges of her senses, which threatened to burst into an explosion of everything that her body could summon up. She wanted desperately to plead with him to let her alone, but he went on.

"Decent people... decent people... I never hear more. You call yourself decent people? Everyone in the yard know your tricks. You think you could send the preacher to jail just because you have a policeman for a boyfriend?"

His remark jolted her and he saw her flinch. So the yard already knew. It remained now for the preacher to come out with that solemn face of his and look her up and down, but his room was dark, thank God.

"I warning you," she insisted. "One more remark like that and I get a summons for you."

Their voices were getting louder and shriller, and one of the residents finally bawled out at them: "Why all you people don't stop making noise and let a man get some sleep... I have to go to work tomorrow morning, please God."

Still the arguing continued. Everyone had given up the thought of being able to sleep until this thing would come to an end.

"Sleep... sleep... sleep," the voice called out again. "Let me get some sleep... I have to go to work in the morning."

The woman was beside herself with anger at the pushcart operator now. "You know what I goin' to do to you, you worthless scamp? You know what?"

The man jeered at her, "Tell me... tell me!"

"When the magistrate finish with you and he ask me what compensation I want, you know what I goin' to tell him?"

"I don't know," the pushcart man jeered again. "I is a fool... a born fool, so you have to tell me everything in the world... Go ahead and tell me."

She moved closer to him and he could smell the stale odour of rum from her breath as her words rasped out of her throat. "I going to tell him that I want the two wheels from you cart for my compensation. Let me see if that don't keep you nasty little mouth shut."

The man who had cried out from his room for sleep now came into the yard when he heard what the woman said. He was infuriated at her. "You want the wheels from the man cart? You gone crazy or what? You have the bareface to take away a man living? Who you is at all? What you think you is at all? You know what a man living is?"

"I want the magistrate to take the two wheels of he cart, and by God I goin' to get them if is the last thing I go do in this world, so help me God," she said, looking them both up and down, one after the other.

*The only t'ing people in the yard could say bout Mr. Harry was that he was a damned fair man... He was fair and square with everybody, that he mind he own business and he stay outa trouble. Don' trouble trouble til trouble trouble you was he motto or, as he use to say, 'Fair is fair'. He was a quiet man who live alone... No friends, man or woman; he had nuttin' to do wid anybody in the yard. Now some people might t'ink that Mr. Harry had some deep secret, some tragedy in he life, but nobody in the yard could truly say that they know Mr. Harry, they didn't even know he full name, he was simply Mr. Harry, just as Miss*

*B. was simply Miss. B. and Miss Violet was Miss Violet.*

*Mr. Harry born in a town call Point-a-Pierre, and that is where they have all the oil refineries, and he was a little boy when it had a time that all kinda people did want to make a strike because they want a penny more a hour for they work. So they come to Port of Spain, marchin' in; they come by bus, they come by taxi, and they stop at Marine Square and everybody start marching to the Red House because they want to go an' see the Governor. An' Mr. Harry, a lil five year old boy, come wid he mumma and pappa because they aint have anybody to leave he wid.*

*Everybody in Port of Spain start locking up they shop and they store. Everybody say that the 'rioters' comin' in and the town quiet and lock up, so if you livin' in Frederick Street and you lookin' out from you gallery to Woodford Square, you could see all of these people with all of them signs and all of them banners. It had a small man by the name of Butler, and he dress up in the finest suits that you ever see, even if you went to Bond Street in England... He had on a bowler hat, and he had a Bible in he hand and he leadin' all of these people to the Red House to talk to the Governor, a white man. Who ever hear that a white man goin' to come out and talk with them? They get up to the Red House and they say they want to talk with the Governor, and they know the Governor must be there cause it have a big car with a gold licence plate with a big gold crown on it outside the Governor office, and they know that the Governor is the only man what have a car what don't have no number on its licence plate, it just have a big gold crown. So the people go up to the Red House and they say we want to talk to the Governor. The Governor send out a man call he aide-de-camp and the aide-de-camp say the Governor aint want to talk to the people. A woman in the crowd take out she handbag, and some people say she hit the aide-de-camp right in he face when he say she can't see the Governor. Nobody know who push who first or hit who first, but what happen was that they call out the police who was right at the back of the Red House, where Police Headquarters was, an' they start shooting and everybody bust dirt and scatter.*

*That night them people from the South spend the night in Shanty Town, just outside Laventille, and Mr. Harry and he mumma and pappa go with them. That night all the police went into Laventille while all the marchers was sleepin, before they could go back in town the nex' mornin' to try to talk to the Governor... and the police had all of them big stick them and all of them horses and they just ride right through all of them people bustin' licks in dey ass, man, woman and child, left, right and centre, and the followin' mornin' the hospital and the jail was full up. Mr. Harry had only five years but he see this and he remember it well. Mr. Harry never forget the sound of horse hoof, he never forget that one and only sound when a stick crack open a human skull; the only sound he ever hear like that was when a coconut fall and hit the ground. He learn he lesson, and how much time he hear it in school too... Mr. Harry go to Piccadilly school, a school what have a lotta ways to make a boy into a straight pin, though Mr. Harry get to be a straight pin in he own way. So though not too many people in the yard know why he live alone, or understand why he didn't interfere when Miss B. put Tommy to kneel down on the grater, we shouldn't be surprise that Mr. Harry did only want the row over with so that he could go back to sleep... so that he could then get up in the mornin' and go do the white man work.*

*Mr. Harry see the police come rushin' into the shanties pullin' out people, man woman and child, half-asleep, half-naked, and start beatin' them. Mr. Harry learn in he own way that if you want to get ahead in the world you must first learn to go along with it. He talk to people in the yard, he didn't have no friends, but he wasn't a enemy to anyone.*

*But it have another lesson that Mr. Harry learn, because when they went back home, although some of them was in the hospital and some of them was in the jail, and some of them was dead, it had a lot of them who get away and went back to they home town. And the next day after they back home, the same people who lead the police attack on the marchers in Laventille, (a fella name Inspector M. G., a old 'pañol, and a fella name Charlie King, and he was a black man who use to ride a bicycle aroun' Port Of Spain and they use to give him a lotta money and free drink whenever he show up because he could always fix them up when they get in trouble, and a young fella name Colonel W. who use to ride all them parades for Empire Day, and the King's birthday, holdin' a shinin' sword straight up and a cork hat with a lot of white chicken feathers fallin' just above he eyes...) these men come South, join with all the local police, some of them on horseback, some of them come by truck load. They come to Point-a-Pierre lookin' for Butler, but they couldn't find him. This time the people was waitin' for them, and all the people have was a cutlass here, a big stick there, all kind of big stone, and one or two of them had a hunting rifle. So when the police come into the town late that night, the first man who get it, because they was looking for him, was Inspector M. G..*

*Now it have some fellas in Point-a-Pierre who come from them far far bush village, and they could swing a stick from a hundred yards away, and they so good with the stick, they could lick out a man eye and that is the way the first horeseman fall off he horse. Somebody swing a stick and it bust open he eye and everybody could see the blood and liquid dripping from he eye, and he fall down from the horse. And when he fall, it had so much cutlass and so much big stick, and so much big stone that when they finish with he, you couldn't tell if it was a man or if it was some animal from the slaughterhouse.*

*The next man who get it was the young Englishman, Colonel W., and the same thing happen; somebody swing one of them big stick; he fall off the horse, and when he fall off the horse the same t'ing happen, only it was a little bit different, he body look very pretty... You could still see it in one whole piece because one of the people rush up and say hold up, is Colonel W., and he was a good whiteman. They use to like to see him on he horse makin' the horse sidestep and cross-step.*

*The nex' fella, Charlie King, was a different story altogether. He start runnin, and he run into a house, and about two, t'ree hundred people gather aroun' the house and they say, well, what we goin' to do, and somebody say, Well, we have a lotta pitch oil. Why we don't t'row a couple hundred gallon of it on the house and see what happen? So everybody waitin' aroun' the house. Charlie King inside de house, and is one of them houses that is not a house really, is a mud hut that they call a carat because the roof make from a kinda grass that they put on, layer pan layer, everytime it leak or every time you see the sunlight comin' in t'rough a small hole in the roof. All you need to take care of a small house like that is one small match. Fightin' goin' on all aroun', police fallin' left and right, and it look as if the people say to theyself, "Now you on we territory." The people can't understand why one nigger have to shoot or beat or lock up or turn policeman and kill he own kind, and when a fella like that fall to the ground and he horse run way, he didn't have time to beg for mercy. One man say to a policeman on the ground who beggin' for he life, "Say yuh prayers... massa day done," and another, "Prayers, my ass" and bam, quick like lightning, he get it. All they hear him say was, "Oh God ah dead!" But the people knew better, they did learn they lesson at the Red House. When a man fall down from he horse, when you lash him across he jaw, it aint finish there. You have to make sure he will never ride a horse again in he life, and they make sure, they crack the bones in he legs in about five, six places with all the accuracy and skill of a surgeon. One man want to remove all the bones from the fallen mounted policeman with his knife, but time was short. So they left him bawlin, and they join the crowd that was dousing the carat hut with pitch oil, pourin' gallons under the house, and they wait for a minute or two to allow the pitch-oil to soak into the carat. One of the men take a old broom made up from the same carat, soak it in pitch oil, strike a match to it, and t'row it on the roof, and when the flamin' broom lan' on the house, is like if the whole house explode, like if a bomb drop on the carat, and Charlie King jump out of one of the window. The carat was standin' on stilts, bout six foot from the groun' because the place where the people live is swampy, and when the rainy season come, it does have one or two foot of water below the house, and when King jump outa de window, he break one a he foot. And the two, t'ree hundred people say, "Stan' back, man, stan' back, let we see how he go run now," and King try to run here, he try to run there, an' everybody waitin'... They say, "Let him run, let we see how fast he could run... let we see how far he could go... let we see if he goin' to beg we tonight... let we hear how he does beg... let we see if he know how to beg." Charlie King running here, he turn back, he runnin' one foot short, the other foot long, and nobody touchin' him. And when he see how the place surroun' with the people, when he see the faces of the people, and the look in they eye, he start to run back to the hut, where he know that it would be an easier way... to burn up heself rather than to surrender.*

*It have a fella who say, "I don' want to see the ole Charlie King go that way... He too damn bad ... he done gone an' do too much bad bad t'ing to too much people... includin' one of me own flesh-an-blood," and he waitin' for him for years and years. He rush out of the crowd and he try to catch Charlie King before he get back into the hut. A couple of other men rush out of the crowd an' collar the man. They say, if that is what King want to do, don't interfere... Let him go and let him finish off he days there. But the fella say no, he say it aint have none of that, he say they can't let Charlie King go that easy, so the crowd talk to one another and they know that they can't hold this man back, because every body know the reputation of the old C.K., and how he use to go aroun' Port of Spain on he bike with a bull pistle bout a yard long. The old C.K. wasn't satisfy with buying a bull pistle from a store, no. He go to a special butcher in the Eastern Market and get anywhere from half dozen to a dozen privates from the bull, and he carry them home and in the back of he yard he put up a old signboard 'gainst the high wall that separate it from the nex' yard, and he use to drive a nail in the tip of the bull pistle and at the other end he run a piece a wire, and then he tie on a stone to stretch the pistle and let them dry out in the sun. And when he see they get hard and dry, the old C.K. didn't take them to a shoemaker to sheath and cover them, no, he learn how to braid thin strips of leather and make he own bull pistle, and it have a lotta people in Port of Spain who know the taste of that special bull pistle.*

*But it still had a couple of men in the crowd who had some feelin', even for the old C.K., and they ask the man what King ever do to he. "Not me," he say, "but one of my family, a man who was married to my sister. You ever see the glass jar King have in he office at headquarters?" Everybody shake they head. They did hear bout that jar... it was only a rumour, they did hear that the jar had about twenty to twenty-five men's penis pickle in alcohol, and the man remind them of it.*

*"You ever see the bottle?" they ask, and the man's voice breakin' now, he eyes fillin' with tears, he say, "Yes, I see it with me own two eye," and then they ask him, "And you see your brother-in-law toto in the bottle?" And the man say, "Well, no, I can't tell a lie, they all look the same in the bottle." This man did take it upon heself to go to police headquarters to try to find out what happen to the missin' organ when they bury he brother-in-law. He keep this a secret from he sister and he family... Only he and the policeman from the deadhouse where he collect the body know. And when King hear that somebody was curious, he had the man send in, and he show him the jar.*

*"It have only one way to handle rough and tumble niggers... that is lesson number one. Slash with the braided bull pistle across he back and the man feel every tiny square of the checkerboard covering of the bull pistle on his skin. That is lesson number two... Keep your ass out of other people business and you go have all your parts where they properly belong. If I ever see your face aroun' headquarters again... that will be lesson number three... Take a good look. Now haul your ass out of*

*here." And with that he shove him out of the room.*

*The crowd turn once again and the few men who hold him back now release him as they standin' aroun' the hut, completely surroundin' it. The man went up to the flaming house and he pull out King from below the house, and he was on fire. The man had a sugar-bag to protect heself from the fire, and the crowd was a little surprise to see that instead of using the bag for heself, he throw it over King to put out the fire on he clothes, and he say to him, "Boy, I don't want you dead so fast... it have too much bad bad t'ing that you do to too much people. You remember me? You remember my face?" But King was only rollin' 'bout on the groun' groanin, so the man went on, "What we have to do today with you is all of them t'ings that you do to other people!" So he take a big stone and he ask the other men if they want to join him, and it didn't take long for them to make up they minds because they remember everyt'ing now. They take all of the women away, then all of the fellas who had weak stomach somewhere in the back, and they say that they goin' to break not only every bone in he body, but they goin' to break them up in a hundred thousand pieces, and when they say that to King, that was the first time he talk. He beg, he say, "Oh God... have mercy." They look at him with he big eyes rollin' aroun' in he head. The fire on he clothes was out now, and two of them hold down he hand, and two of them hold down he foot and the other fellas take they big stone and they big stick and they break up every single bone in he body, and then, when they finish with him, they take him in the house, although it was burning, and they throw he inside the house. And the next thing he say was, "Oh God, I beg you... I beg you." The man who lead them ask, "You beg me, or you beg God?" and King just repeat, "Oh God, I beg you."*

*Mr. Harry was the nephew of that man. That night, after they send way the women and children from the burnin' hut, Mr. Harry was hidin' in the bushes, and see everyt'ing. It was much later in he life that he come to know bout he father, and then it was too late for revenge. Charlie King was dead. Mr. Harry mother disappear from he life as a child. And Mr. Harry get to be a quiet man who live alone... no friends, man or woman, and he dislike violence. So he couldn't understand why Miss Violet want to take way the wheels from the man cart... why she want to take way the man livin, because he know what that mean to a man... It mean somet'ing like cuttin' off he toto and savin' it in a jar like the old C.K. use to have in he office, and that is no way to treat a man, cause a man is not a man when you cut off he toto or when you take way he livin' from he... he is only a cripple, and that aint fair at all.*

Manko came walking in to the yard. His face looked calm and serene, not from that inner peace of mind of holy men but from exhaustion and humiliation. His entire bearing was one of fatigue from the inner turmoil which had burnt out all the energies and fires which could hurl biblical sermons at unbelievers like whip strokes until they cowered. The pushcart man came running towards him, and taking hold of the long white sleeve of his robe, he told Manko how the woman had stolen his money.

"You remember how you did see me looking for something this morning, preacher... You remember, you remember?" Manko nodded; the man had been busy pulling things out, pushing them back, in a wild frenzy as he left the yard. As they moved deeper into the yard, Manko saw the woman arguing with the man, Mr. Harry, who lived across from them, and as the man saw the preacher emerge from the darkness, he lashed out at her again.

"You ain't satisfy you try to put the preacher in jail, now you want to take way this poor man living... You had better hand over his six shillings if you know what good for you." The man's words stunned her for a moment; things were getting out of hand, as they had all day long. They seemed like one thing one moment, and then they were something else. She had meant it when she told the magistrate that they would have to put her in the mad house if things kept up this way. She was first accused of stealing the man's money, and that was bad enough, but now she was being accused of taking away his living, and she could sense from the faces which appeared in the yard that she had made a terrible threat.

"Better mind you mouth and take care who you accuse of thiefing." She wanted to bring the accusation back to money, and the theft, as quickly as possible. She wanted to threaten the man with a summons and the court, but the sight of Manko and the very thought of the court frightened her now.

"If I was you, I would be ashamed to show my face in this

yard," the man told her, looking her up and down as though the very sight of her was disgusting to him. The pushcart man quickly turned to Manko. "Put she to the test, preacher, put she to the test," he cried. He felt that everyone in the yard was on his side now; she was obviously the culprit.

"I ain't have nuttin' to do with your money, nor your test."

Why was she afraid to be put to the test? Now he was convinced that she had stolen his money.

"You fraid," he jeered at her. "You fraid to let everybody in the yard see that you is a thief."

"I don't want to have nuttin' to do with no Bible and no preacher," she said. Manko listened but said nothing. She looked at him with scorn, and he turned his eyes away. Then she took two steps toward the pushcart man. "Fraid? Fraid what?"

"You fraid the Bible... the truth, you fraid that everybody will find out here tonight that is you who thief my money."

The woman looked at him, her eyes large and glassy. Since when did a man like this dare to talk to her this way? She held in all of her hate so tightly that the corner of her mouth began to quiver and one of her cheeks twitched from time to time.

"Put she to the test," the parrot shrieked from Manko's shoulder. Manko calmed the bird. No doubt she would think that he had taught the bird these words to anger her. The pushcart man, however, welcomed the bird's cry.

"You see how much sense that bird have in he head?" He questioned the people who stood about him, who had already decided the woman would have to take the test. If only it had been someone else, she would not have minded, but she saw herself submitting herself to Manko's holiness and power, she saw herself bowing down to his instructions. He would order her to wash her hands before touching his Bible. He would make her cover her head with a shawl. He would tell her how to sit across from him and together they would open the Bible at random, place the pushcart man's house-key between the pages, then together they would tie the Bible closed with the key sticking out. Manko would suspend the weighted key with one index finger, she with hers, and the pushcart man would push the Bible gently, swinging it like a pendulum. Each time it slowed, Manko would instruct him to push it again, while everyone gathered round in a tight circle of suspense, wordless, holding their breath, while God in his wisdom sent down his right hand to touch the book and make it fall to the ground when the thief was found. She looked directly at Manko and saw again that passive and holy look, but she was not fooled by it. What if out of his own spite and his own desire for revenge he let the book fall on purpose?

"If everybody else innocent, why they don't come up and take the test?" she challenged the others in the yard who stood waiting.

The pushcart man felt pleased with himself, he could feel her weakening, and any minute now she would have to submit.

The man who was clamouring for sleep stepped forward. "I ain't 'fraid... I know that I ain't thief nobody money."

"You see," the pushcart man said sarcastically, "you see *that*, preacher... He ain't fraid." Then, turning back to the woman again, "What you thinkin' about so hard?" he needled her. "Either you hand over my money or you take the test."

"Take the test, take the test!" the parrot shrieked, and the woman looked at Manko and the bird with disgust.

"Why you don't take that stupid bird and drown it somewhere?" she said. But Manko would not speak to her; it was the pushcart man who defended the parrot. He moved closer to the bird, as if to examine its intelligence. It was a holy thing purely through association with a holy man.

"This bird," he pronounced slowly and solemnly, "have more sense in he head than so many people in the world." He extended his arms to embrace as much air as they would contain, and he knew each moment was bringing the culprit closer to her guilt.

Her tiredness had become painful now; she knew she would have to go through with it; she stalled now only to assert something deep within herself that said at least that she could make them wait. "I have to think about it," she said.

"Preacher!" the pushcart man immediately turned to Manko. "You ready?" Manko nodded as he went into his room, placed the parrot on its perch and brought out two low stools. The residents of the yard were all up now, and they sat in a semicircle in front of Manko's door. Several of the children of the yard whined and complained until their parents let them stay up to watch the test, and the older ones looked on at every detail with awe, respect and a strange fright. They had heard of the test before, but they had never seen one carried out; they were both fascinated and frightened by the thought of that huge fist, that hand and finger of God which would come piercing through the heavens and flip the Bible out of the hand of the guilty. They had heard any number of first-hand rumours of that book being pitched yards away on occasion, and there were those who had seen the mighty hairs growing on the hand of God as it came down in His terrible judgement. They would see all that tonight with their own eyes. Sleep had left them all. Two of the older boys of the yard forced their way to the front row; they wished to see God's hand, and when their parents shouted at them, Manko came to their defence.

"You want to see the hand of the Lord God?" he asked them severely. There was something of a threat and dare in his tone; he as much as asked them if they thought they were brave enough to face up to such a revelation of God's right hand! And seeing the fear in their faces, he let two of the boys sit on his doorstep where they could see everything.

The woman looked on with growing hate. Her mouth was petulant; she could feel a little zip zip zip in her cheek, and she tried to order it away. She held her cheek muscles tight and firm, but the twitch still would not go away. Manko wanted to ask her if she thought all of this was his doing, if all of anything was his doing. He thought of those wastrels up on Calvary again who would not listen to him, who would not let him help them, and he wanted to tell this woman now that he could have helped her too, he could have helped her to see good from evil if she had only let him before... Now it was too late, and it served her right. He would carry out his mission with complete indifference, cold and hard. She had no shame before, thought Manko, and she had no shame now. Her face was bold as she faced all of those accusing eyes in whose stares it was all too implicit that they were better than she, and she answered them by becoming more arrogant, more sullen.

The pushcart man raced back and forth getting things in readiness. He brought out a stool for himself and placed it facing the centre of Manko's stool. He doubled up a gunny sack which he used in the rainy season and placed it on his head with its conical end pointing up. It gave him the appearance of a monk dressed in his habit as he moved about. He was amazed, delighted with the way the whole yard had rallied to his side. He had been coming and going in the yard for years now, and there was only the indifferent greeting of 'Good morning' and 'Good evening'. How often had he thought, lying in his cot at night, that he could go to sleep and never wake up, and no-one would ever know or care. He was flooded by a strange new excitement; he was the nucleus and centre of something profound, and all the yard-dwellers looked upon him as some kind of fallen hero who was being restored and placed into his proper perspective.

"Preacher... you ready to begin?" he asked Manko again.

"Yes, excuse me, preacher, I hope you don't mind if we begin; you know that I have to go and do the white people work tomorrow mornin', please God," the man who had volunteered to be put to the test first pleaded with Manko.

"I ready if everybody else ready," said Manko. Then one of the boys he had allowed to sit on his step spoke up.

"Preacher, preacher, I want to take the test, is all right for me to take the test too?" The boy's mother, who stood in the back row, had allowed him to stay up on the understanding that he would be quiet, that he would be seen and not heard. Make yourself invisible, that was her motto for children, and the boy looked up at her as he broke this fundamental rule. If he had been close enough and if there had not been so many people around it would have certainly got him a clout.

"Hush you mouth before I come over there and give you a lick in the head," she threatened. "If you can't sit quiet and mind you tail, I send you to bed, now." But the boy knew that she could only threaten. He was about fourteen or fifteen; as was the companion next to him who turned pale at the request. Manko looked at them both and admired the boy who wanted to sit close to that finger of God which would come closer and hover about the Bible. Had he not felt that way too as a youth?

"Let him take the test if he want to; it have so many young people in the world today who ain't have no respect for anything,"

Manko said to the boy's mother.

She nodded grudgingly. "Alright then... if it don't cause no trouble."

Manko told the boy he would go second, then he motioned the man to sit across from him. The pushcart man also sat down and placed his bucket of water in the centre.

"Bless this water and make it holy," he intoned, his voice taking on the reverence and seriousness of the occasion. Manko took the great Bible and held it to his bosom, he closed his eyes and turned his face to heaven, and everyone bowed their heads in solemn reverence as he whispered a prayer, washing his hand in the water as he ended. Then he ordered the men to do the same, and they followed.

"You have something to cover your head in the presence of God?" Manko asked the man after he finished washing his hands. He rummaged in his pockets and drew out a handkerchief, tied four knots into its corners, then slipped it on like a cap. Manko then looked at the pushcart man who adjusted the gunny sack higher up on his forehead and the preacher nodded.

"You close your eyes now and open the book," he commanded, placing the great Bible with its wooden covers between them.

The woman, who stood with one hand on her hip, cleared her throat and shifted from one foot to the other. "It look as if we going to be here the whole night," she said in a disgruntled tone. Some people shushed her, others simply looked her up and down, and she let out a long pained sigh. If she was trying to anger Manko, or to get his attention, she didn't. He was too wrapped up in the severity of his mission.

The man's fingers trembled as they reached out to open the Bible. It was fairly dark in the yard and only those close by could see his fingers trembling, but no one said anything; it only added to their sense of the power of God. But he wondered why his hands were trembling, what he had to be afraid of; he knew he was innocent. He did not steal the money. But the thought that he was going to be so close to that almighty power made him feel strange. It was like going into a church simply to look around and, once there, the presence of God brought to your mind all of the evil that you had done. You entered boldly, you wanted to see the host and the crucifixes, the stained glass windows and smell the incense, that was all, but all of the past began to race through your mind, and you were not so bold any more. He opened the book in the middle, and then the pushcart man handed his house key to Manko who dipped it into the bucket of water, dried it, then placed it between the pages of the book and together they tied the Bible shut. The pushcart man held the book at the bottom, supporting its weight, until Manko and the other man suspended the key with their index fingers.

"By Saint Peter... by Saint Paul... Mr. Harry thief this money," Manko intoned. Then he nodded to the pushcart man who pushed the Bible gently.

The book rocked back and forth. Everyone drew closer, leaning upon one another to get a closer look at the centre and fulcrum of the scene: the fingers of the man and the preacher, and Manko intoning, "By Saint Peter... By Saint Paul... Mr. Harry thief this money," and each time he made the pronouncement, the pushcart man nudged his Bible to keep it swaying back and forth. As they approached the tenth time of the intonation, everyone became intense and when Manko called out for the tenth and last time, "By Saint Peter... by Saint Paul... Mr. Harry thief this money," everyone let out a sigh and people began talking. That was the way God's hand worked, they whispered to each other. Those who had noticed how Mr. Harry's hands trembled, wondered throughout the test if this might not cause the book to fall to the ground, but in spite of that, God's justice was done and he was innocent.

The tight little crowd slackened and shifted. Some tried to get a better position to watch the test, others hurried to their rooms to drink some water or look in on a sleeping infant so that they could rush back in time for the second test. The man relinquished the stool to the boy who sat on Manko's stoop. He had planned to go right to bed and get some sleep, but now he found himself wide awake and wanting to see this to the end. He was still shaken by the thought that he had been so close to God.

Manko, meantime, removed the key from the Bible. The boy borrowed the handkerchief from the man, who now stood next to him, and he went through the ablutions as he had seen the others do. Manko's movements acquired a new grace, his words took on a special music as he spoke; everything he said was filled with religious austerity. His words were no longer spoken, he chanted them as he moved deeper into the expulsion of evil that evening. The woman, too, became more agitated, and she left the crowd to go to her room for a drink of rum. Everyone stared at her, and feeling all those terrible eyes stabbing at her back, she turned to face them before going into her room.

"You want to come to my room and watch my business? You never see anybody take a drink of rum in his life? Come and watch... come on," she invited them mockingly. Worthless good-for-nothings she thought. They think that I fraid and that I want to run away. But I ain't fraid. She tossed the drink down her throat, licked the roof of her mouth, then had another. Thoughts that sprang to her mind gave her strength. Her own anger bolstered her. She thought how foolish she had been earlier on when she had wept through the streets and, as the rum settled in her stomach, she said to herself, "If God himself come down here tonight, I will tell him I ain't afraid." The sentence played a little tune in her head, and it repeated itself with its own momentum over and over. When she got back to the tight little crowd and they all looked her up and down, she finally spoke the words out loud to no one, to everyone. "If God heself come down here tonight, I will tell Him that I ain't fraid."

Manko looked at her now. "That is blasphemy."

"I don't care," she said, like a child pouting and threatening.

"You will have to answer for that," Manko told her sternly. He wished he did not have to speak to her, he was simply going to be the instrument of God in this test.

"Answer who... eh... answer who?" she said hotly.

Manko now stood up and rage burst through him. He held his Bible in his left hand, and he pointed directly at her with his right, all the weight of his curse upon her came shooting out of his arm and his hand and his index finger as he levelled it at her. "You are evil, and you have sinned, and God will punish you. Your soul is black... if you still have a soul, because you cannot even repent; you do not know how to repent, and there is only one place for you, the hell fires." He turned his back on her and sat back down on his stool, his body shaking and his voice at its end, but seeing the boy's innocent face across from him, he smiled. "You ain't fraid?"

The boy shook his head, but Manko knew that if it was not fear, it was something close to it, and he tried to put the boy at ease as they opened the Bible and tied the key between the pages. "By Saint Peter... by Saint Paul... John-John thief this money," he intoned. The boy's face was rigid. His eyes fastened to Manko's index finger and his, then they travelled to the Bible and the string that tied the pages shut. God was near. He had repeated so many times, thousands of times, "God is here, there, everywhere." He had heard others repeat this over and over, in school, in church; he had heard his parents reminding him and the statement had crossed his mind during some of his most secret and personal acts.

"By Saint Peter... by Saint Paul... John-John thief this money," Manko called out again and again while the pushcart man pushed the Bible, watching it sway back and forth.

The woman lit a cigarette, and she let long heavy trails of smoke spiral out of her nostrils. She felt like her old self again, and she knew this would anger Manko, but the preacher's head was bent, his eyes on the Bible, his fingers and the boy's, as the book moved back and forth. "By Saint Peter... by Saint Paul... John-John thief this money," Manko called out for the last time, this time louder and more slowly than before, as if to give God all the time and opportunity to show his hand, but the Bible remained pivoted in its fulcrum, swaying freely and easily between their fingers.

The yard dwellers let out sighs and the silence was broken once more. The boy got up from the stool with a look of pride; he felt that all their eyes were upon him now; he was a hero, and they would all remember him for his bravery. The man who lost the money put his arm around the boy and pressed his shoulder, showing that he was proud of him and his fearlessness. "You are a man now," he wanted to tell him, and the boy sensed it.

Manko did not have to ask her to sit on the stool. She threw her cigarette aside carelessly and sat down on the stool facing him. The stools were quite low and her dress slipped an inch down her knees and with a sudden impulse she grasped the edges of her hem and tucked them between her calves and thighs. Then she gave Manko one of her nasty looks. The less she had to do with him the better, she thought. She did not want him to order her to do this, to do that, so she plunged her hands into the bucket of water and washed them before he asked.

The pushcart man who felt that he had some say in the proceedings looked her up and down with scorn. It was his money that was stolen, it was he who had pushed the Bible back and forth, and it was his bucket of water. She was too bold; why couldn't she wait and listen to instructions. He looked to Manko for sympathy, but the preacher said nothing. The pushcart man could see Manko's jaw tightening, as though he pressed his teeth hard upon themselves, and in a way he was relieved. He shook his head when he saw the preacher's face, and he took the same stance that Manko did; they were in agreement in spirit, if not verbally. 'Let God be the judge... not you or I', they seemed to say to each other, and the pushcart man nodded his head firmly once more as he watched the woman take out a minuscule handkerchief and drop it on her head, where it settled like a butterfly. The man made a cluck cluck sound as he stared at her with a dumbfounded look; she tilted her head to one side and showed him her teeth. He looked to Manko for help, for some word of admonition, but the preacher's eyes were closed and he was muttering words of prayer to himself, and the man now wished that he was like Manko, that he was in the preacher's place. He would not only make her wash her hands, he would make her bathe, he would make her fast, he would make her kneel on sharp stones until that thing in her, that evil thing, broke open; then she would be sufficiently cleansed to touch the Bible. Manko opened his eyes and saw the tiny piece of white on her head.

"That won't do... You have to cover every hair on your head," he said evenly, as if reading out an instruction from the Bible without glancing up at her again. Mr. Harry, who stood nearby, offered her his handkerchief, and seconds passed with him holding it over her shoulder while she stared at Manko, who refused to return her stare. Finally she sucked her teeth and took the knotted handkerchief and drew it over her head until it came close to the level of her eyes.

"Now you satisfy?" she turned to the cart man, whom she knew she could anger. The preacher did not bother to look at her.

Her face looked strange now that her hair was covered, those great dark eyes lolling about in her skull and her painted lips arching and curling with her hot temper: what did men find interesting in her, the pushcart man wondered; they should see her now.

Manko pulled up the long white sleeves of his robe and he dipped the key in the bucket of water, then dried it.

"Open the Bible!"

"Where?"

"Anywhere."

"Anywhere?"

"She is a born troublemaker," someone whispered at the back of the crowd.

"Anywhere," Manko repeated. She closed her eyes and pursed her mouth and let out a long ummmmmm as she reached for the Bible and opened it. Then she opened her eyes and smiled; she wanted to burst out laughing just then, but something held her back. She watched Manko place the key between the pages and shut the book, then he asked her to tie it together with him, the robbed man supporting it at the bottom as before, until they both had their index fingers firmly under the neck of the key and Manko nodded to him to let the book rest now.

"By Saint Peter... by Saint Paul... Miss Viola thief this money."

"My name is Miss Violet," she corrected Manko, and everyone let out a sigh of disgust. It was his fault, thought Manko, he was not sure of her name, he should have asked her, but he wanted to have as little to do with her as possible. The robbed man nudged the Bible and it resumed its arc as Manko began again.

"By Saint Peter... by Saint Paul... Miss **Violet** thief this money." He stressed her name as he called out the accusation, and she nodded her head sharply, as if to say, 'that's a lot better.'

"By Saint Peter... by Saint Paul..."

There was a loud gasp from the crowd as the Bible fell to the ground, and the woman looked at the point on the key with astonishment and disbelief, then she looked sharply up at their faces, some with their hands to their mouths in shock and horror, and then uttered the first words that came to her.

"It's a lie... it's a lie, I didn't do it," and in a burst of emotion verging on tears now, she turned to Manko, "Tell them... tell them... tell them I didn't do it."

"God was with us this evening, brother," said Mr. Harry. "I see it and I believe it... and it ain't have nobody in the whole wide world who could tell us different!"

The woman looked up at him and great tears were welling up in the bottom rims of her eyes; her voice, which she needed most of all, failed her and she felt like sobbing out loud as she looked at the faces one by one, all stern, satisfied, accusing. Then she turned to the pushcart man whose gesture disgusted her as he rubbed his hands together in anticipation of the return of his money.

"I is not a thief... I never thief nobody their money," she cried out. She could no longer speak moderately, she had to shout out all her words or her voice would come out only in a soft croak.

Manko, meantime, was removing the string and the key from his Bible with the detached air of someone who had just swallowed a shot of rum and wipes his hand across his mouth, distractedly. Mr. Harry, who wanted to get back to bed, asked for his handkerchief; he said please in a voice that had the sound of foregone conclusion. He advised her gently, "Better give back the man his money... He done gone and work hard like hell for it."

She began sobbing openly now, her voice broke and she could only speak in halting, incomplete sentences. She tried to appeal to Manko to tell them that she did not steal the money, but he calmly got up and went to his room to lay his Bible down and peel a banana for the parrot, which reached out its little neck and took it in its beak. He stroked the bird on its neck and then returned outside, where the robbed man was shouting, "Gimmee back my money... I wait long enough... I want my money back."

His voice, too, was filled with emotion; he'd somehow had the feeling that the Bible would drop to the ground and he would have his six shillings at that instant; now there was a delay, it seemed endless. Perhaps he would not get his money from her. He pleaded with Mr. Harry and when Manko came out and sat on his stool again, he pleaded with Manko.

"Tell she to give me back my money... I is a poor man and that is all I want. I want my money back... Preacher... preacher... tell she to give me my money back," and he gasped as if he were out of breath.

"Why you don't give the man he money?" one of the women of the yard called out, and Miss Violet now turned to them all. "Everybody in this yard hate me... it ain't have one single soul who have any feelings for me." She was beginning to feel sorry for herself now, they thought. That was the way rum worked; she was bold enough a while ago, now she was ready to cry and try to get everybody to feel sorry for her; well, she could go and find some of those men friends of hers... Let them feel sorry for her. Why did they have to have their heart-strings tugged back and forth?

Then, as if one of the little dregs of strength, one of the little lost molecules of alcohol found its way into the right corner of her brain, she straightened up her back and shouted at them, her remark aimed at the woman and all the women in the yard.

"Everybody hate me because I pretty... that's why you hate me, you hate me because men love me and all of you who only playin' decent, don't know the first thing bout what decent mean... You rotten... all of you... you all rotten from inside to outside." And with that she reached into her purse and snatched out six shillings and threw them at Manko. The preacher looked at her as he removed the coins from the folds of his robes and handed them to the pushcart man. Then, as an afterthought, she took out another shilling and pelted it at Manko. "Here... that is for you... Put it in your collection with my name on it."

Everybody in the yard was fed up with her now, and the last gesture was too much.

"Why you don't get out of the yard?" one of the women said. "Yes, we have young children in the yard and we don't want them to see all the bad things that does go on before they eyes."

"And who going to move me... Which one of you think that you could make me move out from this yard?" she challenged.

The woman whose boy had taken the test was not one to put up with this kind of threat and nonsense; she dealt with threats by following them through with swift action. This much she had learned about life. Never threaten unless you mean to carry through with it, never let someone push you in a corner after you have issued your command, and then let them taunt you and dare you.

"I going to show you who goin' to make you move out of the yard," she said. "Miss Mabel... Miss Maud... Miss Helen, you coming with me?" she asked, as she walked over to Miss Violet's front stoop, lifted up the stove and took it out into the street. She came back and lifted up the large wooden box on which the stove stood. It was too heavy with pots and pans inside, and while she emptied them all out onto the ground she called out to her husband, "Why the hell you standin' there with you hands in you pocket, you can't see that this too heavy for me to carry?" And now the men joined in helping to remove each chair, table, cup, plate, empty bottles, Miss Violet's clothes, armful by armful, and placing them outside on the pavement.

"Now get out and don't ever show you face in this yard again so long as you live," they told her. Miss Violet felt her whole being collapse. Each load of her possessions being removed into the streets felt like blows falling on her body, blows which landed now here, now there, which she tried to parry, but they would fall somewhere else. Now everything had failed her, even her voice, her tears; she did not feel like crying any more: that too was all spent. She went out into the street and sat on one of the boxes for a while, and then she went in search of the little cripple who she hoped was still in the rum shop. And he was.

"You know a place where I could sleep tonight?" she asked him. The little man smiled and they both left the rum shop together.

*Whatever Miss Violet's thoughts was, no one will ever know, not even the reader. She formulate in she mind the exactness of place and time. She know the very cups, plates, sardine cans that the cripple drink out of, eat on, spit into.*

*So they get into a taxi. "It does cost six cent to go to Tunapuna, but at this hour of night it goin' to cost you twelve cents."*

*"Well, that is the way the world is," the cripple say. "It always happen that when you want somet'ing really bad, the price not only go up but it double.*

*The taxi driver smile. He look at Miss Violet, he look at the cripple and he say, "Well, brother, I didn't make the world, and you didn't make the world and I didn't fix prices for after-hours, but if is anyt'ing I like, is to meet up wid a man like you who understand that although we didn't make up the whole damn t'ing, we have to keep the rules." The cripple laugh. The taxi driver laugh and Miss Violet get into the taxi.*

*The streets fly past, the mango trees, the hibiscus, the coconut palms... The taxi cab driver know that he could certainly please Miss Violet more than the cripple; the cripple know that the taxi driver t'inking that he could please Miss Violet more. Miss Violet t'inking of not'ing. Not not'ing really, as you and I know it, but not'ing, a very special kinda not'ing, like time, or time passing, how to pass time. They t'row out she belongings on the pavement. She had the dress she was wearin' and no more than ten dollars. Now these t'ings, while they so, and while they real, and while Miss Violet know all these t'ings, they wasn't as oppressive as the passing of time. How long this night goin' to be... How long this night go take to pass?*

*The cab driver try again. "It have a girl who look exactly like you and she workin' in the Eastern Market. She your sister? Or your cousin?" The patterns, the circles repeat once again. The cripple know what the taxi driver t'inking, he only want to find out Miss Violet address. Miss Violet own concern linger. How long this night goin' to be?*

*Now, Miss Violet in she own way of understandin' did have a vague and primitive idea that to think about time was somet'ing that have to do with men. Yet, here she was with two men; she could still choose one or the other, it wasn't too late; yet she find sheself preoccupy with sheself and she thoughts. She thought it was interesting. Why it is that only men suppose to think about time, worry about time, get restless about time passin', when what was happenin' before she very eyes, in the presence of two men, was that neither of them even vaguely concern with time, the night, how she would pass the night. She understand this in her own way.*

*The time did pass, the men did not think about time; Miss Violet feel time passin'. The night turn into time; the cripple pay the taxicab driver, he give him a shilling instead of sixpence and they smile at each other, each wishin' the other well. The cab driver was suppose to make a play for Miss Violet and he did. The cripple know that was what he wish but could not have. Yet, when they part company, they did so on the best of terms. The cripple did fully expect him to try, knew he would fail and, havin' understood t'roughout he life this simple act which would arouse in the stupid, the fool, the jealous lover some violence, the cripple give him a shilling instead of sixpence.*

*It was a small yard with a great mango tree in the centre. The earth and the groun' around' the tree was swept and raked of the fallen leaves of the mango tree. The moon was out, and it must've been full, and it must've been directly overhead. The shade cast by the light of the moon through the tree stood beneath it in perfect replica. Beyond was a small thatch hut, its sides open to the elements, to wind and rain, equally so to light of sun or moon, light from without. But it also have another light, light from within, a light burnin' in the cripple hut, the light a man or woman keep burnin' t'rough the night so they wouldn't have to enter a dark room. Miss Violet know men? Man? Light within? Light without? Miss Violet know then time, man, light; it remain only for she to know space, place...*

*They enter the hut with its narrow bed, its tin-can cups, its seashell saucers... All of these t'ings was t'ings in themselves, but not so for Miss Violet. These t'ings mean time, she own time, somet'ing she have to endure so that she could find she way into tomorrow. The bed was time, the tin-can cup was time, the seashell saucers was time, but they was someone else' time, the cripple' time. But Miss Violet no longer see them as t'ings.*

*To say Miss Violet understan' time, place, understan' space would be absurd; she would be the first to deny. If you was to ask she, however, if she understan' men, she would tell you, "I know men." To ask Miss Violet if t'rough knowin' as many men as she know could get she to understan' what the Einsteinian understan' would only make she laugh. To point out to she, as a young ant'ropologis' doin' research in the Caribbean did, as he pay she two dollars and fifty cents one night, explainin' to she that it could indeed be possible t'rough the understandin' of one t'ing – man – men who come to sleep with a whore, that you could understand everyt'ing, Miss Violet only laugh then. Now how long ago that was? She understan' this as she look at the cripple, he back turn to she, as he search for a bottle of rum tuck away under a chest-of-drawers. When he turn to she with the bottle, and both glasses in hand, they eyes meet and the cripple know as a man who rarely make mistakes that he did make a mistake; he finally come face to face with someone who understan' that time passin'. He too was lookin, waitin, hopin' to find that look in the eyes of men sittin' out the long night in he own rum shop next door to the all-night bus stop. He was lookin' for time in the eyes of men and here it was, staring directly at him, and it was from the eyes of a woman.*

*So some moments can turn t'ings into time and time into t'ings. Miss Violet was sittin' on the bed takin' the glass of rum that the cripple offer she. They find they have little to say to each other; they agree, they accept each other's terms and conditions. But now there was a sudden change, as if you could feel the wind change, comin' t'rough the latticework of the hut, not from the north, but now from the south. It smell of the sea, the wind change, the time change, and it now become things. The narrow bed was no longer time for Miss Violet, but place, a place where she would stretch out, lay spread-eagle, crouch on hands and knees, do what ever the cripple ask she to do. She love him for this; it was easier. She endurance and she sufferin, when t'ings become time was infinitely more painful than now, now that all the too narrow bed had become was place. That was pleasurable, that was concrete; it was somet'ing that Miss Violet could feel and touch as she did, texturin' the t'readbare blanket, the humid, damp sheet, the pores, the lumps of the mattress, the distinctive odour it have that she did already smell on the cripple. It was the smell of death; how well she know it. Bodies layin' in the tropic sun for twenty-four hours have that distinct odour, not'ing else smell like death, not even dead bodies, but bodies on they way to that place have a even more distinct odour. Miss Violet did smell it even more strongly in the confine air of the taxi-cab, Miss Violet smell it on this bed, in this night, and it was more preferable, less painful now that the bed was no longer time but place.*

*It have a old saying she remember, try to remember, it have to do with how fast time does fly when you in love or when you havin' a good time and she did understan' then, perhaps she still understan' it, perhaps she memory was going, she never t'ink of it as good or bad, desirable or undesirable, painful or pleasurable. She simply take somebody word for it... But now she understand it if only cause it was happenin' to she, and what more, the cripple too understan' she, understan' this.*

*"You want me to leave you alone here tonight? I have a friend livin' quarter-mile up the road and I could go and sleep by his house tonight." She believe him, she had never been compromised and she wouldn't compromise sheself now. She would give him everyt'ing, she as much as say so already; and it break somet'ing fragile in she. She did come face to face with sheself before one of them mirrors that you meet in dreams, where you hold them interminable conversations with youself. She find sheself before that mirror, only this time she wasn't conversing with sheself but it was with this strange and twist-up little man. How sad, she t'ink, to finally find someone else,*

*somebody other than yourself facin' you in the mirror, and how saddenin' to hear them say, "Would you prefer me to go way?"*

*She was t'inking of the preacher, she was t'inking of the courthouse, she boyfrien' the policeman, the magistrate; she was t'inking how she did t'ink of revenge, and she know that to accept the cripple invitation would be a act of revenge, but revenge against what, she now ask sheself? Yes, she did t'ink of sheself, she did t'ink, for example, by the time this night over, one of we will get hurt and she was convinced that it was not going to be she. She didn't consider the cripple and the possibility that he could move back and forth just as the bed move back and forth, now time, now place, and she hear the cripple words all over again, "You want me to leave you here alone tonight? I have a friend livin' quarter-mile up the road and I could go sleep by his house tonight."*

*"You have any more to drink in that bottle?" she ask. And the cripple, who was neither stayin' nor leavin', sit down, uncork the bottle and fill the glasses again.*

*She love him for this. Perhaps what Miss Violet find, what she see in the cripple, and perhaps what he too find and see in Miss Violet mean the same t'ing to both of them. Perhaps they find in each other that t'ing which so many of we lookin' for and never find. He had in he own way change what Miss Violet see as time into something that was no longer time, but place, objects. She was still sittin' on the bed, still texturin' the blanket, examinin' the tin-can and sardine-cans that the cripple spit into – he didn't like to spit on the floor of the hut – the seashell saucers that the cripple eat out of, the bed, they too become t'ings, and not time. It didn't matter that the bed, the mattress, have all its lumps; it did not matter that the smell she know fully well to be the odour of death; it didn't matter that Miss Violet lookin' into the eyes of the cripple who say to she, "I have a friend livin' quarter-mile up the road; I could go up and sleep by his house tonight." It don't matter whether Miss Violet understan' the way love work. If anyt'ing matter, is that these two people find in each other somet'ing that draw them together, somet'ing which alleviate for that moment, that night, some pain, some suffering.*

*Miss Violet get called, named, 'Violet' because she was not dark, not black, not any colour discernable to the eye. Miss Violet get call Violet, a distinction of colour within colour, and she get the name 'Violet' because of that particular shade, shadin', area of darkness, colour that resemble to the unknowin' eye somet'ing approachin' what it ain't have no language for, but is merely a point along the spectrum. She body, to look at it naked, she breasts, to look at them in all they nakedness, she thighs, to look at them in all of they movements, she hips as she stir she pot, all of these t'ings was physical t'ings, part of Miss Violet.*

*This evenin' was different from any other evenin' she know in she whole life. Call it love, call it place over time, call it givin, call it gettin', call it receivin'. Miss Violet lift up she dress; the cripple was sittin' on he chair. He see she legs, inch by inch, as the dress move up, he see the dress go pass she crotch, he see what men did see so many times before: Miss Violet and a thatch of hair between she legs. He see the shape of she hips as the dress go pass, he see that bone, that singular bone that is wider in woman than man. Then he see the narrowness of woman, he see the dress rise, he see she breasts, he see the dress lyin' on the floor, he see Miss Violet lay down on he bed. The cripple begin to get undress. He wasn't like so many people t'ink, somet'ing ugly or grotesque. Or if he was in they eyes, he didn't feel that way tonight. He take off each item of clothin' with a special kinda pleasure and satisfaction in this t'ing, this organism that propel him t'rough the world. He move to the bed. Miss Violet open she legs, the cripple lay pon top of she, he hold she dark and tiny breasts, he kiss them, not like payin' customer, not like a transient, not like the people who come and go out of she life.*

*The cripple know he was a small man. He know even better than the taxicab driver know that he could please Miss Violet more. He never say this to the taxicab driver. Knowledge, truth, love, these t'ings a man keep to heself, and the cripple know that. He find heself as Miss Violet find sheself, in a certain place at a certain point in time where everybody would ask some specific question. But nobody like to ask one question only. Everybody like to t'ink of heself as whole. The world did put Miss Violet belongings, she cook-stove, she clothes, she table and she two chairs on the pavement. Nobody interested to find that simple t'ing that is somebody else, least of all a common little whore. The cripple know this too, because that is the way the world treat him. He move toward she, she spread she legs wide apart and she receive him. They bodies move and writhe, they know that this was some kind of primitive understandin, some way of sayin' to each other that this is not use or abuse, but still they couldn't call it love. He enter she, he feel each and every hair between she thighs, she hold him and when love come and they both t'ink they dying, they know that they find somet'ing special, somet'ing indefinable, somet'ing that other people in all places call love. And they also know that this was somet'ing which was damn difficult to come by, since both of them already know in so many ways, so many times, so many places, where all of this did happen before and they didn't feel so much appeased, but relieved, discovered. They satisfy each other.*

The yard was quiet that night; thieves could have walked in and carried off the chickens and the ducks and no one would have known, for they were all tired when they finally went to bed and blew out their lamps. Even if the parrot had awakened during the night, Manko would not have known. He stretched out in bed, and all of the anguish he felt at Calvary was now replaced by the evening's fulfilment of his belief that God was. He was like a receptacle, sometimes empty, sometimes full; he had only to wait and he would be filled with that glorious feeling that God was near, that God had not abandoned him, that God would show his hand and speak to him. That was faith, he thought, something which was being constantly tried. It was easy now that it was all over, but he wondered where God had been up on Calvary when his listeners turned away from him and abused him. Now that void was filled, and he slept through the night, remembering only dimly when he awakened that old dream of his. He dreamt that his ears had been cut off, and he held them in his hands, only this time he was able to replace them and they clung to his head easily.

As he moved about the room that morning, his body light and free, his limbs moved smoothly and his very vision seemed brighter. The light of the sun playing upon the bleaching stones in the yard, the lemon yellow of the bronze pipe, the earth composed of its millions of eroded pebbles, all came into a sharp focus of light and colour, and he saw them all. The parrot cawed and he went to feed it, revelling in the hues of the bird's feathers, the tiny little eye of the bird, and the way it worked. All of life about him seemed fuller, and within himself he felt, if not joy, then a kind of awakening and clarity, a sense of being aware of all the minutest things about him to which he had been oblivious.

He started brushing his teeth at the pipe in the yard, then stopped abruptly and went through the gateway into the street where Miss Violet's things had been deposited, but they were gone. She must have come before the break of dawn with a pushcart and carried them away so that she would not have had to face any of the yard dwellers. He was glad of that. She had been humbled sufficiently not to want to create more contention, all of the venom, hate and anger that welled up in her had been quelled, and she would be a better person for it. He could see her going about packing up her things docilely, and shamefacedly disappearing into the city where she would relive this night and learn from it that no matter how fast or furiously one lived, one could not forever escape the hand of God's justice. "The longest rope have an end," he mumbled to himself, bringing his thought to a close with final conviction.

The woman who moved Miss Violet's things out on the pavement was busy at her charcoal brazier. Breakfast was over and her husband was at work and her children off to school. She saw the preacher washing and brushing his teeth with an air of abstraction that she did not want to disturb. A man like that must have a lot of things to think about, she felt, but she wanted to do something for him, and since there was still some coffee left and a little cod fish with chopped onions, she began fixing up breakfast for him on a little tray, and when he was finished washing and on his way to his room, she took the tray to him.

"I know that you don't have nobody to cook for you and wash your clothes, preacher, and I want you to know that if you need anything, all you have to do is ask," and as she ended her offer she handed him the tray with his breakfast. "Here, is just a little something that I have leave over from this morning."

Manko thanked her, but she insisted that it was not his place to thank her, but hers, she simply wanted to show him that they appreciated having him in the yard; appreciated the way the preacher handled her son and let him take the test; she was now both proud of the boy and pleased that the preacher had so much interest in young people. Secretly she thought the boy a rogue, an idler, a wastrel, and it was all right for her to think so, she was his mother and that was only natural. The preacher had been able to bring about something in the boy, and perhaps his good influence would help, not only in their home, but everyone in the yard. "God only knows we need somebody like you," she said, "especially nowadays."

He took the parrot on his shoulder and they set off down

Frederick Street. It was getting close to noon and the streets were busy with cyclists and shoppers, children on their way home from school and some clerks already on their way to lunch. The streets were so choked at times that Manko had to wait, enjoying the flow of traffic and the faces of people who nodded to him as they went past with some word of respect. At the foot of Frederick Street the traffic had come to a standstill and none of the cars could move. Drivers leaned on their horns, they got out of their trucks and cars and cursed each other, but as Manko went past, each one of them stopped cursing and they either tipped their hats or they nodded to him. He thought of Calvary again, and decided just then that he would return to the hill and the cross in the evening. He would make them listen. His rum shop was close by and he went in to get out of the din in the streets.

The heat of the day was beginning to climb at this hour, the sun lashed at the streets and the cool fresh atmosphere of the rum shop in its semi-darkness fell upon him as he entered. The sounds inside the rum shop were honed down, people spoke in whispers compared to the grating noise outside. He had not placed his order when he saw a policeman coming toward him, and when he was upon him, Manko now recognized him as Miss Violet's friend.

"Where she gone to?... What you gone and do to she that she move out of the yard and nobody know where she move to?" Manko ignored him, the bar attender came and Manko called for a nip of Black Cat with a lime and some sodawater. He looked straight ahead, as though he did not hear that he was being spoken to.

"Preacher, I talking to you man to man now. Forget I have on a uniform, I only asking you to please tell me where she move to... just tell me..." and his voice began to choke up. The rum, thought Manko. Everything about this huge hulking man annoyed him. He remembered how brazen and cocky he had been when he delivered the summons, then again how he had collared him in the Court House.

"He was playing God," thought Manko, and then, "A man ain't have no right playin' God. He should respect God."

"So you lookin' for Miss Violet." He looked him straight in the face now, and the policeman seemed ridiculous. His eyes were swollen and red, and when he shook his head in answer they seemed to loll around in their sockets.

"Well, Miss Violet ain't looking for you." The policeman stumbled back a step as though he were pushed and in his drunkenness he would have lost his balance had not Manko reached out and grabbed him by the shoulder to steady him. The parrot almost flopped off Manko's shoulder and it began to shriek the last words it remembered, "Put she to the test... put she to the test." And now all the people in the rum shop were staring at them; they saw the preacher's hand on the scruff of the policeman's neck and they took another swift shot of rum before they looked up again to make sure that what they saw was real. Manko was now shaking him by his collar. "You ain't have no respect for anything... no respect for this uniform you wearing... no respect for yourself You looking for Miss Violet, eh! The woman ain't want to have nothing to do with you, and you ain't have no shame, no shame at all. Get hold of yourself, man, get hold of yourself."

The great bulk of the man began to shake and tremble, and now tears were in his eyes. The more sad he became, the more Manko despised him. The bar attender ran back and forth because several customers were calling for their checks; they wanted to pay and get away. If there was anything they could not stand it was to see a man crying, such a huge man too, a policeman at that, and of all places in the world, in a rum shop. The bar attender was in a state of panic, the rum shop was in a state of chaos. He tried to take people's money and give them their change, then he tried to persuade the policeman to leave, but the man stood there as if lost to the world, frozen to his boots. Then he tried to placate Manko, who was stern and stony-faced, and now the din from the streets became cloying and the horns of all the cars pitched above their voices, making everyone shout even louder because the traffic had come to a complete standstill. The bar attender moved about like a mad man, muttering, "I only have two hands you know... I only have two bands you know." Every now and again this soft muttering would burst out at top pitch as he addressed it to someone who wanted to get away, clear away from people crying in a rum shop.

"Why you don't get out there and do you work... You standing up here like you dead!" he told the policeman, lashing him with words which only made his tears well up into a bigger and bigger pool in his terrible eyes and roll down his cheeks. Even Manko could not bear the sight of him, he looked away most of the time, but the man stood like a child crying, "I want Miss Violet... I want Miss Violet." Then, as though everything had failed him, he fell to his knees with his hands clasped in the position of prayer at the preacher's feet, and he looked up at him with imploring eyes, and he said to Manko, "I beg you, preacher... you hear me... I beg you... tell me where Miss Violet gone to."

"Get him out of here. Carry him outside in the road," some of the men still left in the rum shop cried out. It was more of a cry of anguish, their voices *were* filled with loathing and disgust because there was something spreading about the rum shop like a disease and any minute now they might catch it, and the only person in the rum shop who could end it was the preacher, because he stood stern and sober.

"Why you don't carry your friend home and let him cry it off there?" someone cried out again in the same pained voice. 'Friend,' thought Manko, and the word nettled him. He turned to look over the half doors of the bar where all the noise still rang out, and now two drivers had gotten out of their trucks and were ready to start fighting. Manko grabbed the policeman by the scruff of the neck, just as he had been grabbed in the court, and he hauled him outside where he shook him vigorously on the pavement, and then, not satisfied with that, he dragged him into the middle of the road and began working his arms like a puppet going through the motions of directing traffic. Everyone wondered what was going on, but the traffic had started moving, and they hopped into their trucks and cars as the policeman stood with long tears running down his cheeks, his arms moving by themselves now, while Manko stood on the pavement.

"Worthless good-for-nothing scamp," he said as he walked away.

He set out for Calvary Hill, stopping to look back from time to time over his shoulder, and he could still see the policeman directing traffic, he could see his terrible face again, the worthless scamp. Big and bad when they have the upper hand, and then the next minute crying like a child for, of all people, Miss Violet.

'Please, preacher, please, please preacher,' he mimicked. 'I beg you preacher, I beg you.. tell me where Miss Violet gone to!... 'I'll tell you where Miss Violet gone to... she gone to hell where she belong... worthless... heedless...' They have hard ears, they hear the voice inside they bosom, but still they won't listen. I'll make them listen if it's the last thing I do in this black world." People brushed past the preacher and saw his mouth moving as he spoke to himself; he strode along heedless of everyone and everything.

*In the meantime, this is what happenin' in the Chinee coffee-shop where Manko headin'. The place wasn't just a coffee-shop, it was a parlour, and most of the parlours in Trinidad run by Chinee people who they bring to the islands to do sugarcane work when the freed slaves refuse to work the plantations. Hot-sun, hard-work, sickness. It look as if everyt'ing work against them Chinee people; they die off like flies, and they had to bring in people from India to save the plantations, but although some of them went back to China, it still have plenty Chinee people in the Caribbean, and a lotta times they have a small shop or a parlour, and they livin' in the back.*

*The Chinee parlour was a small hole in the wall; this one have two hole in the wall – you could call them doors if you like. Is only that you never see the doors, except on Sunday, when everyt'ing shut up tight tight tight. The parlour was always dark no ass, and you always feel cool in that darkness. Is a good place to get out of the hot sun, a nice place to relax your brain in the city, a nice place to get a cold coke or a big bottle of Solo orange. It cost the same price like coke, but it have two times the amount in a Solo.*

*Like all of the parlours in town, this one have a small wooden counter, and on top of the counter it have a small glass-case with Chinee people food... something call* POW *that look like a big white jumbie-parasol, a mushroom, and inside this jumbie-parasol it had either chop-up meat or a black kinda paste that taste sweet and sour. A lotta people don't like to eat the one with meat because they hear it say that Chinee people does eat cat and dog, and that is what it have inside the jumbie-parasol. Below the counter it had a old rusty Coca Cola cooler with the Solo and cokes in it. The doors use to slide across the top when it new, but this one see better days. The owner just get a fifty-pound block of ice and put it in every morning and he put a bucket to catch the water when the ice melt. Behind the counter it had a lotta shelves with all kinda glass jars with stoppers, the kind you don't see too much of nowadays, and inside the jars was candy, fortune cookies, sweet prunes, and salt prunes that come straight from China. All of them wrap-up nice in little packet bout an inch square, and the packet have a picture of a beautiful Chinee lady – only she face – and in the backgroun' it have a picture of some nice lookin' mountains, with a blue river flowin, and then a lot of Chinee words that maybe the owner heself didn't know how to read.*

*The owner livin' in the back of the parlour like all them Chinee places, and when you see the sun get hot like hell, the Chinee man pull out he bed halfway, so that you could see he foot, whilst the rest of he behind the curtains where it nice and cool. He was a tall man, and everybody call him Tall-Boy, but in front the parlour it have a small rusty sign with he name on it:* **The KOW*LOON CAFE... Chong Sing, Prop.** *People who didn't know Tall-Boy just call him Chin, like they call all Chinee people. That is the way in Trinidad; everybody have to have a name, and if you have one foot shorter than the next, they call you Hop and Drop because of the way you walk. If you like to talk a lot, you name Big Mouth, or if you get to be that age round fourteen or fifteen when you is all hand and foot and you body is just beginnin' to turn into man, they call you Big-Foot, or somebody would say, "What happen, boy? It look as if when God passin' out foot, you run up first." And if you get christen' that way, you live with that name for the rest of you life.*

*Tall-Boy was only half-sleepin' on the army cot he use for a bed so that he could wake up if any customers come in to do business. Five boys come in the parlour, and he wake up when he hear the juke box start up with some steel band music. They order Solos and pow and the salt prunes in the little packet. When the record over, they put in more money and they play the same steel band record again, and one of the boys holdin' onto the juke box like he holdin' onto a woman, and he gyratin' he body like loose ball-bearings. Tall-Boy only waitin' for them to leave so he could catch a little shut eye. Sun so damn hot is all he could t'ink. One of the boys ask for a snowball, and Tall-Boy shave some ice and pour some red syrup on it, then the boy ask for a spoon, and when he finish the snowball he begin beatin' out the rhythm of the steel band music on the metal table with it.*

*The boys keep orderin' one t'ing after another, and one of them who had the little packet with salt prunes begin to tear up the little envelope in tiny tiny pieces, lettin' the confetti fall on the floor. Then, when they put in more money to hear the same steel-band record, they begin to dance in the parlour, jumpin' up an' down on the tear-up picture of the Chinee lady. By this time so, they play the record bout twenty-t'ree time, and somet'ing happen to the man as he see them jumpin' up an' down on the picture of that beautiful Chinee woman. He put he left hand on the counter and swing over.*

*"Get out!" he scream at them, and he pull out the plug from the jukebox. The boys lookin' at one another until one a' them say, "What we do, man... We ain't do nuttin'... we is good customers." And another boy say, "We money good like anybody else money... It ain't have hole in it like Chinee people money."*

*Tall-Boy just say, "Get out!" He finger pointin' to the street. The boys back away a little, and one of them, who was standin' up on the pavement, read the old sign: L. Chong Sing, Prop., and he say, "Mr. Chong Sing... who' happen to Mr. Ping Pong?" And they all laugh like hell because they know that the way a Chinee man get he name is that when he born he poopah and he moomah t'row a tin can up in the air, and when it fall down an' it make a sound like Chong Sing, that is the way the Chinee baby get christen.*

*Tall-Boy only lookin' at the tear-up pieces of paper with the woman picture on it. "Get out before I call police!" he shout again.*

*Then one of the boys who standin' up on the pavement outside sing out, "Chinee, Chinee never die... flat nose and chinky eye," and now all the other boys join in the song, over and over, over and over, until Tall-Boy make a quick dash, but the boys quick like lightnin'. Tall-Boy run out on Queen Street and he grab the shirt tail of one of them. Tall-Boy begin to shout, "Hold them... Hold them... Police!"*

*Just then Manko turn the corner onto Queen Street and see the gang of boys comin' and one of them run straight into him, and the preacher collar him firmly, while the others run off in different directions.*

"Hold him... hold him... Don't let him go!" the storekeeper ordered Manko. Manko held a firm grip on the boy's collar. He looked at the boy and the boy looked at him with surprise; he was one of the boys from the yard.

"Don't let him get away, preacher. I want to get a police to lock them up," the proprietor shouted as he came out of the store, his fingers and knuckles white in the grip he held on the shirt tail of the other boy, who Manko now saw was also one of the neighbour's sons, the boy who had taken the test.

"They come in here right after school and they play ONE record... just one record forty-nine times. When I tell them that if they play it one more time it go drive me crazy, this little vagabond here..." the storekeeper broke off to clout the boy on his head, taking time to catch his breath, which was coming short from his anger and excitement, "this little rogue here curse my mother and my father, and he put in the money to let the record play again."

Both of the boys looked sheepish; if it had been someone else they would have tried to scramble away, but they knew that they would have to face up now; word was sure to get back to their parents. They looked at Manko with guilty, pleading faces, and the storekeeper went on. "When I tell them to get out of my shop, they say that they have to hear their record, that it is their money, and this one here..." he clouted the boy hard on the head again, "this one here is the biggest rogue and the ringleader."

Manko shook the boy he held onto with all the rancour built up in him. "You hear what the man saying? Is true?" he asked, knowing full well that what he had heard was only half of the taunting the group of them must have inflicted on the storekeeper.

"Forty-nine times... forty-nine times," the storekeeper kept repeating incredulously, as though he could not believe how he had been able to withstand the din and the noise all that long. His eyes were fixed on the jukebox, which had sounded like thousands of savages had broken loose and were striking on every unearthly tin cup, church bell, oil drum, bamboo pole, old automobile rim, and above all that, there were hundreds of voices, wild as a batch of animals stalking through the jungle... This was the fiftieth time, and he could still not believe it.

"I don't know what happening to young people nowadays... Where they get so much money from... Where they get so much money to waste."

At the mention of money, the boys looked quickly at each other and they both turned pale. Manko saw them look at each other, then quickly at him, then away, and the boy he held onto now bowed his head and began fidgeting as Manko's face, too, turned pale. He stared at the storekeeper, then he stared at the boy he held onto, and his mouth fell open, his throat went dry, and he felt as though someone had struck him in the pit of his stomach. He wanted to speak, but his voice failed him, and he suddenly felt a sharp tug, and the boy he held onto burst away, leaving his shirt in Manko's hand. He had been unbuttoning his shirt buttons surreptitiously as he held his hands in prayer in front of him. The empty shirt fell to the ground as the boy raced away, and finally a deep groan escaped from way down in the preacher's lungs, as he felt his body go all limp and weak, as though that was his final exhalation.

"Is you..." he began, but could not finish. The boy looked at him with a cocky smile now. Whether he was being cheeky or whether he knew that it was all in the open now, Manko could not tell. He laced his fingers together tightly and came down on the boy's head with all the force and strength in his arms, and as the boy flinched under the blows, the storekeeper began to plead with him to stop.

"That enough, preacher... Leave the rest to the police... to his parents."

"Oh God!" Manko cried as he came down with the last blow, and the storekeeper now let go of his grip. The boy raced away, dodged a couple of people who tried to grab him, knocked over two garbage pails on the pavement and then turned into Charlotte Street and disappeared.

And now Manko moved through the city like a bird, his robes flying, his feet moving him along. Decision had fled, and so too had anticipation; he moved now through pure instinct, not knowing where it would take him. The streets chose him, they beckoned him, and when he turned corners they too seemed to wrench him in the direction they wished, and he felt pushed along by a great tide which threw him up at the foot-hill of Calvary, where he could see the great gold cross reflecting the sunlight. He moved up the zig-zag path wearily, and only when he reached the summit did he feel any peace or possession of his thoughts. The workmen who restored the image of Christ were just taking the bust into the small chapel for the night, and one of them elbowed the man Manko had made to repent at the foot of the cross.

"Look... look who coming up the hill... You friend."

"My friend?" the man inquired, looking at the figure of Manko at the foot of the cross now.

"Your friend, man... your friend... Gentle Jesus meek and mild." The other workmen had teased him about the way the preacher had made him go down on his knees and repent, and sometimes during their lunch break, as they sat about the little summit eating or drinking or playing a game of wapee for a few pennies a hand, one of the men would shout out in the middle of the game, "For I am a sinner," and the other men would shout in chorus, "For I am a sinner!" Then he would say, "Ignorant of thy ways," and the others would repeat with a straight face, as though they were in a church service, repeating the pronouncements of the minister, "Ignorant of thy ways." And before long, the workman who had been humbled at the foot of the cross by Manko would fly at them, trying to rain blows left and right, but they would all subdue him amidst gales of laughter, and then they would let go of him and all dash away like a group of small boys who had had their fun.

They stood for a while in front of the chapel with the bust of Christ, almost completely retouched and repaired of the obscenities written on the feet, the missing toe, the missing ear; vandals had, indeed, driven real nails into the feet of the image. All had been repaired and the image was almost ready to be replaced on the cross. The workman looked at the beautifully finished bust and then he looked to the foot of the cross where Manko knelt, his hands clasped in prayer, his head bowed one moment, looking up to heaven the next.

"The foreman gone home yet?" the workman asked. He wore a tight little grin on his face, and his comrades knew that he was up to some mischief.

"Yes... he gone home," one of the men answered. They all

pretended they would stay on the job until five o'clock, but whenever the foreman left for the day, one of them leaned over the runner of the summit and made sure that he had left for good, then they began washing up their brushes and putting away their plaster and paint pots, then they took the bust into the chapel for the night and went home.

"Come on, boys... let we get rid of the Good Lord and wash up and go home," one of the men suggested, as they all waited with the image supported by them all: at its feet, head, its outstretched arms and about its middle.

"No, man... wait... You don't want to be saved? You don't want to go to heaven? What wrong with all you fellas at all? Here we have a chance to find out the way to heaven and all you could think about is going home. Come on, let we see if the preacher could show we the way." His voice was teasing and cajoling, and he spoke in whispers so that Manko would not overhear them. They walked on tip-toes now as they took the image into the chapel, speaking in whispers which bound them through its strange magic into accomplices to some rude joke which no one fully knew.

When they came out of the chapel and one of the men was about to padlock the doors by slapping hard on it, the others all hissed, "Shhh!" Then they began following the leader on tiptoes through the small enclosure at the end of which stood the cross, Manko at its foot, his head bowed. They heard him muttering to himself, but they could not tell what he was saying. The workman who led them on cocked his ears to try to catch some word or sentence, but he could hear nothing, and when he was upon Manko he bent close to the preacher's ear and shouted with all his might:

"REPENT, FOR THE KINGDOM OF HEAVEN IS AT HAND!"

Manko's body reacted like a coiled spring. He jumped to his feet, stepped onto the pedestal of the cross and stood there with his arms outstretched, his face hung to one side, and his eyes almost closed.

"And I am a sinner, Lord... unworthy of they holy works!" cried Manko, as if truly in agony. Lorrito, the parrot, was also startled. It was perched on the preacher's shoulder as he knelt, and when he leapt to his feet, the bird rose with him and continued upward as Manko came to rest on the pedestal. It now sat on the top of the cross, making loud screeching noises. The workmen looked at each other as they searched their minds. Did they think it was blasphemy for a man, a plain ordinary everyday man to get up on the cross like that? Or was it funny, ridiculous, laughable? They stood around the cross, not knowing what to make of Manko.

"He get half-cracked or what?" one of the men finally asked. Manko's head was still turned to one side, he refused to look down at them.

"Why you don't come down from the cross and stop playin' the fool, man!" another said, but the one whom Manko had humbled was not keen on having him come down, he enjoyed seeing him up on the cross.

"How long you goin' to spend on the cross? We have to start work tomorrow, please God," he jeered, and now they were all pleased to see the sprawled body move a little, as though it were coming back to life.

"As long as it take for me to repent and be taken back by the Lord God."

"He **must** be crack," said one of the workmen. "Listen... Repent for me too while you there, you hear?" another said, and they all laughed.

"And suppose you drop asleep in the night, and you fall down from the cross and break a rib?" the ringleader teased on, enjoying the sight of the preacher with his sad look on his face, all sprawled out on the cross. His fingers were beginning to curl and arch out, and the man was about to ask him if he would like to have a few nails driven into his palms to help him stay on the cross.

"Help me brother!" cried Manko, "I have sinned against the Lord... Help me!"

The men were still confused by the entire episode. Everything had happened so quickly, no one knew what to do. It was not the kind of thing that happened everyday. They laughed from time to time, but their feelings changed from one moment to the next. If someone had said, "Let's crucify the worthless scamp... That is what he want," they might well have gone along with it. And it was the ring-leader whose suggestions and provocations set up the direction.

"So you want we to help you stay up on the cross 'til morning come?" he teased on, the others waiting to hear what would come next. It would be something to tell their children in their old age.

"Help me, brother, I need your help," Manko repeated as the ringleader slipped away without the others noticing. When he returned he brought a stepladder and a length of rope.

"Let we help this poor man to repent," he said to the others, as he set up the ladder beside the cross. The rope was already well tied around Manko's arms and legs as he was bound to the cross before he began to protest.

"That's right... Go ahead... Crucify me!" he screamed. "You did it before... Go ahead and do it again... Crucify me!" The men were ready to race away, but they waited for the ladder to be put back in the chapel, and when the ring leader emerged to take one last look at Manko, the preacher called out again, "Crucify me!"

The man looked to his comrades who were a short distance away, and he called them back. "Come on man... you ain't hear what he want. He want we to crucify him, he won't be able to feel good unless we help him."

There were two garbage pails on the edges of the summit and he drew them close to the foot of the cross as he called to his comrades, and when they were all gathered there they pelted the contents of the garbage pail at him, then they raced away in gales of laughter. Manko groaned and sighed as each piece of refuse struck him, and the bird jumped off the cross as each piece missed it, then it returned to perch above Manko's head after they left.

Towards two o'clock in the morning, a policeman was making his rounds on a bicycle and he heard groans coming from the summit. There were all kinds of tales of ghosts and jumbies who inhabited the place, and no one ventured near it after dark. The policeman looked up to the cross and he thought he saw a slight movement there. He turned his eyes away to refocus them, to make sure that he was not dreaming. Then, when he looked again he saw only the small silhouette of a bird on the shoulder of Christ, shrieking, "Caw... Caw... Caw."

## JENNIFER RAHIM

*Songster and Other Stories*

Rahim's stories move between the present and the past to make sense of the tensions between image and reality in contemporary Trinidad. The contemporary stories show the traditional, communal world in retreat before the forces of local and global capitalism. A popular local fisherman is gunned down when he challenges the closure of the beach for a private club catering to white visitors and the new elite; the internet becomes a rare safe place for an AIDS sufferer to articulate her pain; cocaine has become the scourge even of the rural communities. But the stories set thirty years earlier in the narrating 'I's' childhood reveal that the 'old-time' Trinidad was already breaking up. The old pieties about nature symbolised by belief in the presence of the folk-figure of 'Papa Bois' are powerless to prevent the ruthless plunder of the forests; communal stability has already been uprooted by the pulls towards emigration, and any sense that Trinidad was ever edenic is undermined by images of the destructive power of alcohol and the casual presence of paedophilic sexual abuse.

Rahim's Trinidad, is though, as her final story makes clear, the creation of a writer who has chosen to stay, and she is highly conscious that her perspective is very different from those who have taken home away in a suitcase, or who visit once a year. Her Trinidad is 'not a world in my head like a fantasy', but the island that 'lives and moves in the bloodstream'. Her reflection on the nature of small island life is as fierce and perceptive as Jamaica Kincaid's *A Small Place*, but comes from and arrives at a quite opposite place. What Rahim finds in her island is a certain existential insouciance and the capacity of its people, whatever their material circumstance, to commit to life in the knowledge of its bitter-sweetness.

**ISBN 13:9781845230487**
**UKList price: £8.99 US$19.95 CAN$24.95**

**NEW 2007**

## LAURENCE A. BREINER

*Black Yeats: Eric Roach and the Politics of Caribbean Poetry*

For readers of West Indian literature, a study of Eric Roach requires no justification. He is the most significant poet in the English-speaking Caribbean between Claude McKay (who spent nearly all of his life abroad) and Derek Walcott. Roach began publishing in the late 1930s and continued, with a few interruptions, until 1974, the year of his suicide. His career thus spans an extraordinary period of Anglophone Caribbean history, from the era of violent strikes that led to the formation of most of the region's political parties, through the process of decolonization, the founding and subsequent failure of the Federation of the West Indies (1958-1962), and the coming of Independence in the 1960s. This book presents a critical analysis of all of Roach's published poetry, but it presents that interpretation as part of a broader study of the relations between his poetic activity, the political events he experienced (especially West Indian Federation, Independence, the Black Power movement, the "February Revolution" of 1970 Trinidad), and the seminal debates about art and culture in which he participated.

By exploring Roach's work within its conditions, this book aims above all to confirm Roach's rightful place among West Indian and metropolitan poets of comparable gifts and accomplishments.

Laurence Breiner is the author of the critically acclaimed *Introduction to West Indian Poetry*.

**ISBN 13:9781845230470**
**UK List Price: £17.99 US$34.95 CAN$43.95**

**NEW 2007**

## TRINIDADIAN WRITERS FROM PEEPAL TREE PRESS

**James Christopher Aboud**
**Kevin Baldeosingh**
**Faustin Charles**
**Mark De Brito**
**Brenda Flanagan**
**Anson Gonzalez**
**Vishnu Gosine**
**Cecil Gray**
**Ismith Khan**
**Rabindranath Maharaj**
**Lelawatee Manoo-Rahming**
**marina ama omowale maxwell**
**Ian McDonald**
**Sharlow Mohammed**
**Lakshmi Persaud**
**Jennifer Rahim**
**Raymond Ramcharitar**
**Eric Merton Roach**
**Sam Selvon**



---

Peepal Tree Press, 17 King's Avenue, Leeds LS6 1QS, UK
Tel: +44 (0) 113 2451703
E-mail: contact@peepaltreepress.com